Bitter Rivalry

SM REINE & HEATHER HILDENBRAND

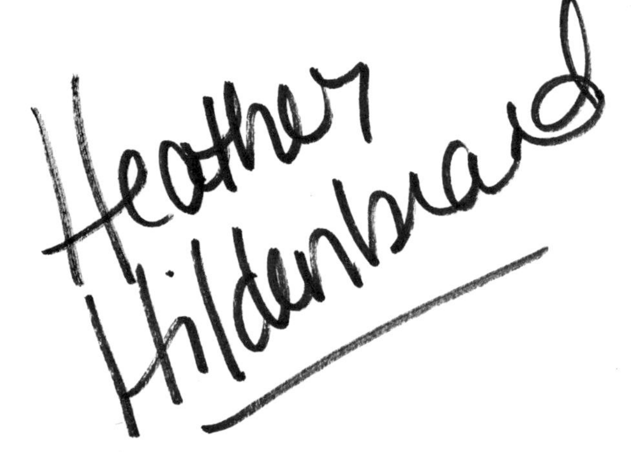

Editing, Kristina Circelli, Red Road Editing
ISBN-13: 978-1979843812
ISBN-10: 1979843813

Series Reading Order:

Bitter Rivalry
Bitter Beloved
Bitter Truth

~1~

CHARLIE

High school dances were overrated. Sweaty perfume, crepe paper, and a whole lot of trying too hard all in the same room. What was the point?

I shifted my weight and fidgeted with the lace on my sleeve. Again. Why did I come here? Joey Lusk aside, school dances weren't my scene. I'd spent more time hiding in the corner than on the dance floor.

But when Joey asked me to come, rumpled brown hair in his eyes, every other word being, "um" and the beginning and ending something like "if you don't have anything better to do," how could I have said no? I was futureless, not heartless.

Besides, my mother had been acting so weird

lately, any excuse to get away was a good one. She had always been a little high strung, but this was a new level of crazy. On top of shortened curfews and a cell phone with a wide-range GPS tracker, my mom was making me practice shape shifting to my wolf form on a daily basis. We hadn't practiced that together since elementary school.

Back then, I'd needed all the help I could get controlling the animal side of myself. As a young child, any temper tantrum or missed nap was enough to send me over the edge. I'd once thrown a fit in the grocery store when my mother had told me no over a candy bar and cried so hard, I'd sprouted fur. My mother picked me up and carried me out wrapped in her jacket. We ate canned soup for dinner that night because my mom was too scared to risk going back.

Being a shifter—a werewolf as some would call it nowadays with the whole paranormal craze going on—wasn't exactly an easy life. Especially when your first and only priority was keeping it a secret. I cringed to think what life would be like if people knew I had the ability to grow paws and a snout at will. I hated the spotlight as it was. Whether that was a product of genetics or a built-in security measure after years of living with my high-strung mother, I wasn't sure.

The music blaring through the speakers changed to something more like techno and I cringed all over again. Techno was not my thing. Neither were dances. Or any organized social functions. My list of friends was pretty short and none of them were close. It sucked—but not as much as it would suck to find a bestie and leave her again when Mom decided we'd worn out our welcome in this town. I never knew when the end was approaching until it was too late. Last time, she'd already packed the entire house and had the moving truck idling at the curb when I'd returned home from school.

There was no time for goodbyes with an unpredictable life like mine, which meant there was no time for friends, either.

Joey brought me a Styrofoam cup full of punch that tasted like powdered mix and water. Someone had thrown in a cherry to fancy it up, but it was wrinkled and pruned from sitting too long in the juice. "Thanks," I told him, forcing my words to sound cheerful.

"No problem." He smiled and stuck his hands into his pockets. "Are you having fun?"

"I am." My tone wasn't convincing.

His brows knitted in real concern. Joey was a nice guy. Where most kids had given up and begun to ignore me, he'd always said hello. Always been around. He wasn't … hot, but he was kind. Way more points for that, in my book.

"What's wrong?" he asked.

"It's nothing. I'm just not feeling very well." I hated lying, but I couldn't help it. I needed air. Open space. Somewhere without walls and crowds of people. "I think I should probably get home. It's getting late anyway."

"Just let me get the car and I'll take you," he said. He looked disappointed, but since it probably didn't occur to him that I might be dishonest, he seemed more concerned about me than with the date being cut short.

"No, Joey, its fine. I can manage. Besides, Kassie Gordon asked me to make sure you saved her a dance. You can't leave without dancing with her." I pointed to where Kassie was sitting on the set of bleachers the staff had left out for the occasion.

It was dotted with a few girls who were unlucky enough to rank below me on the social ladder. Kassie spotted us and waved from her seat, a shy smile on her face that allowed a small peek of the metal lining her teeth. She met Joey's gaze for a second before getting flustered and busying herself with smoothing out her cream-colored skirt.

"Kassie wants to dance with me?" Joey asked.

"Very much. And it will make me feel better if I know at least one of us gets to have a good time." This part wasn't a lie. Joey deserved to have fun and he deserved it with someone like Kassie—someone who he'd have a shot at a romantic future with. Someone who could agree to a second date.

I, on the other hand, was future-less.

I made a quick exit, happy to see Joey returning Kassie's shy glances before I slipped out the gym door. I paused on the front steps of the school, trying to pick a direction. The pavement was wet from a hard rain earlier in the evening, but the sky was clear now. I breathed in deeply through my nose. One of my favorite things about moving to Kallypso, Oregon had been the myriad of earthy scents. On dry days, it was all dirt and wind, but tonight, after a fresh rain, everything smelled wet and heavy. It would've been delicious even if I hadn't been a wolf—or so I told myself.

I knew I should do the human thing and walk home, like any other kid my age would do. It wasn't far, a little over a mile. But the forest that edged the parking lot to my left was calling. I couldn't resist.

I bounded down the steps and darted in among the parked cars, heading straight for the tree line at the edge of the blacktop. I glanced around as I ran, making sure no one witnessed my strange exit—you never knew who'd step out the gym door to sneak a cigarette—but my senses told me the coast was clear.

I sniffed once more to be sure. Yep. I was alone.

The moment I stepped off the pavement and onto the soft soil, my body relaxed. A collective exhale of the stress and anxiety brought on by the dance. My muscles swelled and strained and I gave in eagerly to the shifting.

The change was fast and easy these days, but it wasn't always that way. It was kind of embarrassing as a kid. Lots of torn clothes and nudity. But there was a trick to it, and my mom and I had practiced enough that everything went much smoother these days. Now, I knew how to shift at will—and still have my clothes on when I shifted back.

I held my breath and focused on keeping everything together as I shifted into my wolf form. Skin and muscles rippled. The air around me shivered. I fell onto all fours, and when my hands landed, it was paws that hit the ground instead of fingers.

Starting out with an easy run, I increased my speed. Faster and faster—until the depressions of my prints were so slight, they barely left a mark. I'd been denying myself this all week. It was too difficult to give in often here, among so many humans. But tonight, with the rain to mask my scent, and all of the nocturnal creatures hiding from the deluge, I could run. I gave in to my stolen minutes of guilty freedom and let everything fall away but my wolf.

The run home was entirely too short, but at least I made curfew. I shifted at the edge of the woods, bracing against the chill of the night air on my bare skin as my fur fell away. My dress remained intact, though a little muddy around the hem (which would annoy my mom to no end). The shoes weren't so lucky. I must have left them behind.

"Stupid heels," I muttered. For whatever reason, dress shoes were so much harder to hang on to than sneakers.

I stomped toward the house, a cottage rental we'd been lucky to find so far into the school year, my bare feet sucking in and out of the mud as I went. Halfway up the back steps, voices drifted over. I halted mid-step and looked around for the source.

"I'm telling you, I just scented someone, and it wasn't Anita," said a male's voice. The speaker sounded young, close to my age maybe, but it wasn't anyone I recognized.

"Must be on foot, then," said another. This one was deeply male. Older.

I tried to place it too before their words sunk in and I realized what they were saying. They smelled me? A human couldn't have, which meant only one thing…

No way. It couldn't be.

I'd never met another shifter. Mom said they were out there, drifters like us just trying to fly low, but something about the way she'd said it always made me think she knew more. The few times I'd pressed, she'd snapped back at me.

"They're dangerous. All of them," she'd almost yelled. "They can't be trusted."

"I'm sure they can't all be bad—" I'd said but she'd cut me off, eyes blazing with something I couldn't name.

When she'd spoken again, I'd known better than to argue it. "If you ever see another shifter, Charlie, turn and run."

I shook the memory of her words away. But I couldn't do that now. Not with her somewhere inside.

I dropped into a crouch and huddled behind the rhododendron bush my mother had planted when we moved in. It was enormous already, but provided enough peepholes for a view.

Two figures stood close together at the edge of the yard, where the driveway met the sidewalk. Their voices had dropped to a whisper, and I could no longer make out what they were saying. They took turns gazing left and right down the darkened streets as if searching for someone. From the looks of things, they still hadn't spotted—or scented—me in the backyard.

I was suddenly glad I hadn't bothered with shoes. I shifted my weight and felt the sharp edges of the mulch pressing into the soles of my feet. I winced. The front door opened and closed and, for an agonizing second, I was terrified my mother had come to investigate. But a second later, I heard a male's voice call out a greeting and another dark shape joined the first two. Their voices stayed hushed but no one made any moves to conceal themselves.

My heart pounded against my ribs.

They'd been inside my house.

My mother hadn't come out, which meant she was still inside. What did they want with us—with me? How did they know her name? I wanted to believe they were friendly, but after my mother's warnings and the way they didn't speak or move as they waited, I wasn't convinced.

I had to get past them. My mother was in there, and I wasn't going to abandon her.

"If she doesn't get here soon, we're going after her. This is taking too long," said one of the men, the older one. The other two grunted an agreement.

They wandered closer and my pulse thudded louder as I realized they were headed straight for me. I took one last breath and held it, afraid of making any noise, and crept up the back stairs and into the house.

It was pitch dark inside. My mother always had lights burning. Lots of lights. She always said darkness was deceiving and she wouldn't be deceived again. I'd asked her to elaborate on the remark, to no avail. At this point, I'd given up.

Mom was … Mom.

The back door opened into the kitchen so I went through there first. The passage of every silent second made me tenser. Why couldn't I hear Mom? Why were there no lights? I tried the switch and got nothing.

I crept out of the kitchen, listening for any indication our visitors had decided to wait inside after all, but heard nothing. The dining room was empty and dark as well. I turned down the small hallway, toward the front of the house. A sliver of light shone from underneath the office door. My mother kept her computer in there, but she mostly only used the room when she paid bills or filed records. What the heck was she doing in there now?

I stood outside the door, shoulders heaving with silently labored breaths. I raised my hand to the knob and then stopped. What would I do if there was someone else in there? Should I shift? Had they?

I'd spent too many years' carefully hiding my true nature. I couldn't risk shifting and showing my hand now. I needed to protect myself as a human. I glanced around the empty hallway for something to carry. All that sat close by was a floor lamp and an end table filled with odds and ends—car keys, unopened mail, and a paper clip. Nothing that would help me. As I moved, a floorboard creaked underneath my feet.

"Charlie, is that you?" my mother called from inside the office. Her voice was high-pitched, twisted into some octave I'd never heard out of her before. That, more than anything else, scared me.

The knob squeaked and twisted. My breath caught in my throat. I wondered frantically if I should run and hide or stay and fight, but there was no time. The door opened to reveal my mother, her light hair backlit by a lamp that gave it a soft glow.

Her face was shadowed and I squinted to make out her expression—was it worry or fear she wore as she faced me?

"Mom? Are you okay?" I asked, my words coming out too fast in my panic.

"I'm fine." She spoke calmly enough, but her eyes gave it away. She teared up and her chin trembled. Something was seriously wrong.

"Mom," I said uncertainly, "there are men outside. They were trying to—"

"I know, honey. We've been waiting for you." Her voice cracked and I could swear her tone was apologetic. What was she sorry for?

The heat of alarm spiked up along my throat and into my face. "What's going on?" I demanded.

She reached out as if to touch or comfort me, but at the last second, she pulled back and pressed her fingertips to her trembling mouth. "Honey, I'm so sorry. So, so sorry." Her tears spilled over and ran down her cheeks.

A floorboard creaked behind me. Something swung in my peripheral vision and made contact with the side of my head. The crack echoed in the quiet, and I felt myself crumpling like an accordion.

The last thing I saw before it all went black were my mother's tears, falling.

Falling…

~2~

REGAN

Footsteps sounded and I looked up a full ten seconds before Carter appeared. I knew it was him by the weight of his boots. My ears pricked at the sound of his familiar footfalls, and my mouth went dry. If Carter was back, it could only mean they'd found her.

I blinked and Carter materialized, his broad frame filling the office doorway. He looked at me first but his expression was fixed, unreadable. His light hair and blue eyes were striking, though not nearly as piercing as that cold stare he always wore when he faced my father. Even at seventeen years old, pack warriors were expected to be soldiers. And soldiers followed orders. No room for feelings or opinions.

Despite that, Carter had been my friend for as long as we'd both been alive. We'd been born a month apart—he never let me forget he was older. And despite our penchant for arguing like siblings, he was one of the few I trusted these days to see bits of the real Regan. But he also liked to mess with me and I knew he was purposely ignoring me now. Ass.

I bit my tongue as he turned to my father across the log cabin-style space.

"She's here," Carter said.

Those two simple words made my pulse accelerate. I looked at Dad, and he looked at me. My excitement was mirrored on his weathered face.

It felt like I'd been waiting for my sister to arrive for days, even though it couldn't have been more than a few hours since the retrieval party left. That might have been because I really had waited for her my entire life.

I grew up hearing stories of her: Charlotte Vuk, the estranged pack member who had grown up around humans. They said I would meet her someday—never a specific date or anything, just a vague "someday" that could have been in a year or a hundred years. Until then, all I had of her was a description ("she looks a lot like you," Dad said) and a photo I'd hidden from my mother. My chest ached as I realized even that had changed. I didn't need to hide it so well anymore.

Sometimes at night, when I couldn't sleep, I laid there and tried to imagine what this Charlotte was like. Was she as tough as me, molded by a childhood as a pack heir? Did she like hunting too?

Was her favorite color red? With all of the bad blood between our elders, could we ever be friends? Could our shared DNA actually, finally mean I'd have a friend? Someone to tell secrets—even weaknesses—to? It was a lot to hope for.

Now I was finally going to meet her.

It was all I could do not to leap to my feet and hug Carter, who had delivered the news. But I kept my feet carefully rooted. Despite being one of the top warriors in the pack, Carter backed up when Dad stood, giving him the deference the alpha deserved, and kept his head down. I was the only person who didn't have to show submission around Dad, since I would be his equal soon. Future alphas never bowed.

"Where did you put her?" Dad asked.

Carter replied with his eyes on the floor. "In the room we prepared. Just like you asked."

"Good."

The single-word answer revealed nothing. I didn't know how Dad could react with such control. He marked his place with a bookmark, set the volume on the table between us, and strolled toward the door. His movements were unhurried—casual. Inside, I was dying with impatience.

As soon as Dad was far enough away, I jumped up. "What is she like?" I whispered.

Carter shrugged. "Unconscious."

"How revealing," I said and Carter grinned wickedly.

"Fine," I said, "Don't tell me anything. See if I help you next time your long list sibling returns."

Carter snorted.

The door swung shut. I hurried through it to catch up with my dad. He walked into the fresh morning air and I stuck close to his back, trying to keep my expression schooled. The rest of the pack knew something was up. They got out of the way when Dad and I passed, hurrying to do their daily tasks, but I could feel them watching. I kept my expression blank as I walked; I couldn't look nervous or excited. I had to keep my cool. That was what an alpha did, no matter what, and after everything that had happened in the past few days I knew my future was almost upon me.

Thoughts of my mother crept in but I shoved them out. I couldn't think about her now, with everyone looking to me for the future. I couldn't afford to break down. Maybe later—when I had some privacy. Dad said leaders never cried. Mom said they only cried in the dark.

Charlie's room had been prepared in the main house, where we—the alpha family—lived. But Dad didn't lead me to the bedrooms upstairs or even the guest room at the back of the first floor. Instead, he led me down to the basement.

The only thing down here was storage. A large room lined with books and trinkets given as gifts from various celebrations. And a small room off the east wall that was rumored to have been used as a prison cell before our jail was built.

Confusion tinged with dread washed over me as I descended the stairs. "What—?" I started to ask, but then I saw the guard at the bottom of the stairs and stopped.

They had put my sister in a locked room.

"Just a precaution," said Dad.

This time, the lack of emotion in his tone made me wonder. Maybe he wasn't as thrilled as I was after all. My dread flared into worry. Was there something they weren't telling me?

"A precaution against what?" I asked.

Dad didn't answer, but I guess he didn't really need to. Our werewolf pack had been at war with a coven of vampires for over a century, and there was a lot of bad blood on both sides. We had faced assassination attempts more than once. This last one succeeded. My mother ... But I couldn't think about that right now.

Maybe a locked room was a good idea. The basement was more secure than the rest of the house. But the guard Dad has assigned, a muscly ex-military guy named Brent, didn't fill me with confidence. What was the saying … All brawn and no brains?

Brent snapped to attention when Dad stopped in front of him. "She's awake," he reported.

My heart skipped a beat.

"Don't let anyone disturb us," Dad said, and then he went in the room. I had to take a deep breath before following him inside. My pulse pounded in my wrists as my adrenaline spiked, like I was about to go into a fight instead of meeting my long lost half-sister.

I followed Dad into the shadowy space and stopped.

There she was.

Charlotte Vuk was sitting up in bed, staring at the small window at the top of the wall beside her small cot. The black bars broke the morning light as it spilled over her. Seeing her was almost like seeing a reflection of myself, but the subtle differences were powerfully disconcerting. She was really pretty, with luminous brown eyes and cascades of thick brunette hair we had evidently both inherited from Dad. Her olive skin and full lips were just like mine.

That was where the similarities ended. She had plumper cheeks than mine, and a few extra pounds on her hips, curvy like a girl should be where I was slim and toned. And she smelled weird. Simultaneously familiar and yet ... strange.

She was also wearing a pretty blue formal dress. It was kind of ... frilly.

Frills. I tried not to gag.

I stayed behind Dad, folding my hands behind my back so I wouldn't shake.

"Charlotte," Dad began in a warm, friendly voice I had never heard out of him before.

Charlotte swiveled to face us with a jerk of shock. Hadn't she heard us come in? Could her senses really be that dull? Tendrils of disappointment crept into my heart. "I'm so glad to see you. I've waited so many years."

"It's Ch-Charlie actually. Who are you? And where am I?" Her voice was softer than mine. More feminine. But underneath that, I heard the fear. My senses opened and I caught the subtle tremble of her chin, the small scent of panic on the stale air. Terrified, more like.

Dad stepped forward, always dominant no matter the situation. "You know who I am."

Charlotte's eyes flicked between Dad and me. Recognition dawned on her face. "You're ... him. My …" She trailed off as if unwilling to finish the title. "I've seen pictures, but..."

She moved like she was going to get out of bed and go to him, but he didn't budge, and she didn't make it any farther than throwing her legs over the side. His separation was palpable and surprised even me. I could read Dad better than anyone. Up until today, he'd been excited to meet his youngest daughter. The few moments he seemed uncertain I'd chalked up to nerves. Why was he suddenly so closed off?

At his hesitation, Charlotte's hands clenched tight in the bed sheets. Her eyes, already red and puffy, filled with tears. Not the stoic facade of a wolf with alpha blood. My excitement dropped another faction.

"I hope the retrieval team didn't scare you," Dad said. "We had to get you out of there quickly. There was no way of knowing who might be watching."

Charlotte shook her head like she wanted to argue but had already given up. "Where's my mom?" she asked dully.

I shifted uneasily. Shouldn't she know the answer? Hadn't someone already explained? This was getting more and more uncomfortable.

Dad sighed and shook his head. "She can't come here."

"Why not?"

"Your mother and I..." He glanced at me and Charlotte's—or rather, Charlie's—gaze followed.

Charlie and I didn't have the same mom. A couple of months after my mom got pregnant with me, my parents went through a rough patch. At least that's how Mom described it. My dad had spent some time running patrols with his old girlfriend from high school, one thing led to another, and baby number two was conceived. My mom didn't say much else, except that for reasons I was "too young to understand," Charlotte and her mother were sent away "for their own good."

Dad didn't say much about it because it made Mom too mad. The little bits I knew of Charlotte were mostly eavesdropped conversations or slipped-up details given by my father or some other elder in the pack. Now, after what happened to my mom, maybe I was finally going to get the whole story.

I waited for my dad to explain, just as curious and clueless as Charlie.

"Trust me when I say it's safer this way," Dad said with his typical mysteriousness. "There are people who remember when she used to be here, and our kind can hold grudges for a long time."

Charlie flinched. "When you say 'our kind,' do you mean...?"

"The wolf pack."

Charlie blinked and I could practically feel her disbelief in the exaggerated movement of her eyelids. "This is nuts," she said finally. She pushed the sheets back and stood. Her legs wobbled, but even as she steadied them, her eyes narrowed. Off-balance, uninformed—what had they done in order to bring her here?

I glared at Carter, who hovered in the hall

behind me, but he remained fixed on my dad.

"I want out of here," Charlie said. "I'm going back to my mom. I have friends, you know. I want to finish school. I have to—"

"You'll be educated here," Dad interrupted. "The things you learn here will be different, but more practical than any outside education system."

"You have schools here?" Charlie asked, brows raised.

"We don't have schools like the humans do," Dad said. "Our classroom is the forest. Your classmates are other pack members. Your lessons will be the animals you hunt."

Her jaw fell open. "Hunt? As in, kill stuff?"

Dad narrowed his eyes and his next words sounded accusatory even by my standards. "I know you've been sheltered from many things, living with humans, cut off from us. You have so much to learn in a short amount of time. But this is what you were meant to do, Charlotte. This is where you belong."

To her credit, she didn't back down under Dad's stare, like so many others. She lifted her chin and glared at him. "Don't I have a choice in the matter?" she asked.

"Duty is more important than choice," Dad said and for the first time since I'd laid eyes on her, my heart went out to this lonely stranger who was my sister.

Duty *was* more important than choice, or at least I'd heard it so often, I could almost believe it. But Charlie hadn't. She was so new to this world, clearly, and I could only imagine the panic and confusion she must feel being ordered to give up—

well, everything—and just matriculate.

Charlie chose that moment to look at me and I had to force the sympathy out of my expression. Her gaze was a little desperate, like she wanted me to help, but I couldn't go against Dad. Not even for her. I looked away.

"Duty to what?" she said, staring at Dad again. There was a stubborn note to her voice that reminded me of myself. "This isn't my pack."

"It could be," Dad said.

Charlie narrowed her eyes. "What do you mean?"

Dad hesitated and then explained, "You're in line to become alpha, Charlotte."

It was like a punch to my gut. I drew in a hard gasp as all of the air was sucked from the room. "What?" I squeaked.

Dad shot a glare at me, and I immediately felt guilty for even that small outburst. I clamped my jaw shut, but I couldn't shake the betrayal and confusion from my expression. Luckily, Dad ignored that and turned back to Charlotte. She was looking back and forth between him and me, and seemed even more confused than I was.

"Regan's mother," Dad gestured to me, "the pack alpha, was killed recently. The law says the role must be filled by a female of the Vuk line."

"But…we have different mothers," Charlie blurted and Dad's mouth quirked.

"Yes, thank you for pointing that out. Pack tradition dictates that the line is taken from the male, the father. But it can only be passed to his female offspring. You are both my daughters and less than six months apart." My eyes flicked to Charlie and my cheeks flamed in indignation. I'd always known that's how it'd happened but seeing Charlie digest it all made it somehow worse.

Dad cleared his throat and went on. "Since you share the same birth year, pack law dictates the terms very clearly. Where two possibilities exist, there will be a contest. The winner gets the position of alpha, first in command. The runner-up will gain the role of beta, or second."

Behind me, Carter made the smallest of sounds. I glanced back and found him staring angrily at my dad. He caught me looking at him and his expression smoothed out, calm and blank. I faced forward again, unwilling—and unable—to take on his stuff right now. I was having a hard enough time with my own.

I felt my hands ball into fists at my sides. It was all I could do not to scream. I bored holes into Dad's head, but he didn't turn. He probably knew I was trying not to flip out, but he was more concerned with Charlie right now. She was staring at him like he'd just spoken Russian.

"A competition? For alpha?" she asked. She shook her head and then nodded her chin in my direction. "And I have to compete against her? Who is she?"

Dad smiled. "Charlotte, I would like you to meet your half-sister—Regan Vuk."

"Half-sister?" Charlie's voice caught on the word "sister," and our eyes met and held.

It seemed like an extra charge of energy traveled between us, and for a second, I felt like we were both feeling the same sordid batch of emotions.

It made me feel a little strange that she hadn't known I existed when I'd spent my whole life dreaming about her. I had wanted to know her, to have her companionship, for so many years. And now that I'd finally met her, she didn't have a clue about me. And to top it off, the very first thing we would do as sisters would be to fight. She would see me as a competitor instead of a friend.

I felt more than just a little disappointed. I felt played.

It didn't matter by whom. Mom, Dad, the Universe. They had all known and yet none of them had told me. And here I'd walked into today thinking I'd gain an ally.

Charlie broke her gaze from mine and looked back at Dad. "So, Regan and I are both…you're my father," she said in a small voice. Finally. Almost tripping over the last word.

"Yes," Dad said.

Charlotte stared up at him for an extra beat. He'd managed to keep his answer short and devoid of any emotion. Even I had no idea what he was thinking.

"I want to talk to my mom," Charlie said.

Dad nodded. "You can call her anytime you like. I've arranged for you to have this." He pulled a cell phone out of his pocket and handed it to her. "Everyone in the pack has one. It works as a two-way radio as well. Just hold down the button and let us know what you need. Someone will always respond."

Charlie took the phone and pressed a few buttons as if to test it. She looked back at Dad with a hint of defiance. "And if I try to leave?"

"We will always bring you back," Dad said. His voice was firm, leaving no doubt he meant every ounce of what he said.

Charlie's expression heated. "Like you brought me here? Threatening my mom, knocking me out?"

Dad ignored her but again, it made me wonder what they'd done to get her here. "This is your home now. It's easier if you accept that now."

"I guess I don't have a choice," she said quietly.

"We've prepared a room for you, upstairs in the main house. If you're ready to accept your new role, I think you will be more comfortable there."

He waited until Charlie nodded and gave a mumbled, "Okay."

Dad's heel scuffed the floor as he turned and strode briskly out. "Show her to her room," Dad said to Brent. There was a mumbled reply.

I hesitated, wanting to offer something kind or more humane than the exchange I'd just been a part of. But my mind was incapable of forming the words. Dad's announcement still echoed: a contest. Charlie and I would duel for alpha. My future was no longer set. And even though I knew logically that it was due to pack law, I couldn't help but blame the girl standing in front of me for taking it all away. For threatening what was rightfully mine.

I was supposed to be alpha. Me. Not her. And Carter was beta. It was unspoken between us but it was there. Even if she were the friend and sister I'd always dreamed of, she was still my opponent. But now there would be no way to know. If I wanted to win, I had to stay separate. I couldn't allow myself to get close to my enemy.

With that in mind, I cast one last glance at Charlie and then followed the others out.

~3~

CHARLIE

The house smelled like pine cones. I had no idea why or how I knew that from the depths of the basement, but there it was. The scent of woodsy spices and polish grew stronger the farther up and out I went.

I'd barely made it up the staircase before curiosity got the better of my panic. Rather than focus on how I came to be here and why Mom would fail to mention this place—and this family—to me before, I paid close attention to how I felt being in it *now.*

Regan and my father—that still felt weird—disappeared out the front door just as I stepped clear of the basement stairs. I listened to the latch click and had just enough time to blink into the cheery sunlight filtering through muted curtains nearby before my guard—Brent?—grunted at me.

"This way," he said, and I fell into step.

The cell phone became sweaty in my tight grip so I slid it into my pocket and left my hands free as we crossed the foyer. I did a quick sweep at an intersecting hallway but there was nothing but stained wood in every direction. Brent veered right toward the stairs and I followed, one ear cocked and listening for sounds of anyone else at home, but everything was quiet.

I ran a fingertip along the paneling as I climbed, studying the designs and markings carved into the bannister. They felt old—ancient and important in a way that only my intuition could understand. I shivered and dropped my hand.

My room turned out to be surprisingly plush, in a cabin-in-the-woods kind of way. The wall panels were dark wood decorated in framed art with lots of greens and yellows that reminded me of woods without a single picture of a tree. I had my own leather couch—the fancy kind without the arms—and a bed that could have fit half my high school class in it at the same time.

And it was squeaky clean. Just like the foyer and stairs, I remembered. I'd hate to be the one stuck with dusting in this place. Whoever it was, they were good. Even here, the underlying scent of spice and pine ruled in a pleasantly subtle sort of way.

But even though all of that was nice, it wasn't me. It wasn't my room, or my house. None of this should have been my life. Or maybe, in a twisted kind of way it should've been mine, instead of that Regan girl. But it wasn't. It felt foreign. I missed the smell of my room. The sound of my mother piddling around the kitchen. The grandfather clock in the hall, ticking away an afternoon. This place was nothing like our cottage. It was nothing like home.

In the doorway behind me, Brent threw my duffel bag onto the bed and left without another word.

"Wait," I called, but he was already gone.

I was tempted to try the doorknob to see if it was locked or not, but it wouldn't have really mattered, either way. I had agreed not to leave. And even if I did, they'd made it very clear what would happen if I tried. There would be people waiting for me. Watching. I was as good as shackled to the room, lock or no.

I gave the room another quick onceover, my gaze landing on my bag. Now that I was alone and clearly here for the duration, my soiled dress suddenly felt heavy on my shoulders. There'd been nowhere to change along the way. Funny how that happened when you were unconscious and kidnapped. And now, after having slept in it, the straps had dug into my back and left uncomfortable red marks. No lights were on, but the tempered sunlight from the single window was more than enough to illuminate the mud damage to the skirt. I held it up and groaned. It was even worse than I'd suspected.

"No more white tags," I muttered to myself,

thinking of how my mom had tried to talk me into the sale rack that day at the store. And how my babysitting money hadn't let me hear her.

I explored my way around the bedroom and was happy to find the small door on the far side of the dresser led to a tiny bathroom with a stand-up shower. I washed faster than I ever had—terrified Brent would return and get nosy. But no one came and my dripping hair chilled me enough that I almost cried with relief when I found my favorite worn pajama pants in my duffel. Maybe Brent wasn't all bad after all.

Once I was dressed comfortably, I sank to my bed, looking at the cellphone my dad had given me. According to him, Mom was just a phone call away. But even as I tapped absently at the screen with my thumbs, I couldn't bring myself to dial her number. She must have known about this for years. My dad, the pack, their plans for me—the more I remembered her expression just before they'd knocked me out, the more certain I became. My mom had known they'd come for me. And when they did, she'd let them.

She probably wouldn't have chosen this for me, but had she stood up against them and said no? I doubted it. My mom was a lot of things, but brave and bold wasn't on the list. So I threw the phone on my pillow and flopped back, staring at the way the light played on the ceiling and pretending I didn't care that my long-lost dad was somewhere in the vicinity. Or that I hadn't lain awake at night my whole life wondering who or where he was—and why he wasn't there with me. Now I knew. He was busy ruling a werewolf pack in … I had no idea where I was, actually. But wherever it was, Mom wasn't.

I had to choose. Get to know my dad. Duke it out with my new sister for an alpha spot of some sort. Or try to sneak home to a mom who'd been lying all along about the one piece of myself I'd always wanted to know.

It wasn't fair. Any of it.

Someone knocked on the door. I didn't move or respond, and they knocked louder.

"What?" I snapped.

The door opened, and I caught a sideways view of light-brown hair and large chestnut eyes that reminded me of my own before recognition speared through me. I shot upright as Regan stepped inside.

We stared at each other for a long, silent moment. I hadn't gotten a chance to take a good look at her in the basement, but now I studied closely the shape of her face, her stiff shoulders, and the way she seemed capable of commanding invisible armies with that death glare of hers. She had short brown hair and a too-serious expression, like she was already a leader, even though she couldn't have been much older than me.

My sister.

I wish I'd known I had one before today. It might've given me a leg up on what the heck to say. I felt uneasy under her gaze, like a bug on a microscope's slide. Something about it pinched a nerve and my frustration spilled over.

"What do you want?" I asked.

Instead of getting angry, she dropped her eyes

and paced around the room. "This is nice. Dad gave you the big room. You should be happy."

"Happy?" I barked out a bitter laugh. "I should be happy that I was kidnapped?"

Regan stopped in front of a big panoramic painting on the wall. I hadn't noticed it was there until she gave it that same long, hard stare she had been giving me. It was a picture of open grassland, and wolves—normal or otherwise, I couldn't tell—were chasing down a mountain lion. It was bleeding from bite wounds on its flanks and rump. It didn't look like it had long to survive.

She turned, arms folded behind her back. There was something distinctly formal about the way she stood. "Our father is taking care of you."

"He's done a real good job taking care of me for the last seventeen years," I said. Part of me felt bad for pushing her but she was so … blank. I couldn't help but poke at her.

"What was it like?" she asked, surprising me into confused silence with the question. "The outside world, growing up out there, I mean," she said, turning back to me with open curiosity.

"It was … normal," I said with a small shrug. Then my brows furrowed at how vague I sounded. And before I could stop it, the honesty came spilling out. "I mean, it kind of sucked sometimes. My mom always made us move around so I never stayed anywhere long enough to make close friends. Now I know why," I muttered. "And I didn't have a dad or … friends," I finished. I'd almost said siblings but caught myself. She didn't need to know I'd always wondered what a brother or sister would be like.

"Sounds lonely," she said.

"Sometimes," I admitted, more grateful than I was willing to let on that she actually understood me so easily. "But sometimes it was great not worrying about compromise or pleasing everyone else's agenda. And when I need time alone to think, I got plenty of it."

Regan sighed heavily enough that I looked up. She wore a wistful expression and said, "Now that sounds nice."

Silence fell between us and while the unspoken friendship bloomed, I couldn't shake the feeling that this might be the nicest moment we'd ever have. Especially if this contest thing was for real.

"We're enemies, aren't we?" I asked finally.

"What?" Regan's brows lifted and she blinked, but not before I saw the truth in her eyes.

"Enemies," I repeated. "I mean, this is nice and all, you coming to my room and making friendly conversation. But in the end, if our father was telling the truth, we're competitors. Not a great way to start off a solid sibling relationship."

"Dad wasn't lying," she said, almost defeated. "We'll have to compete for alpha."

"But can't we come up with some sort of compromise. I mean, if you and I both agree to refuse—"

"You can't refuse, Charlie. It's pack law," she said in a lecturing tone that grated on me.

"Pack law," I said, nodding. "Of course. And I know so much about it that I totally get why that's such a big deal."

Regan sighed, which pissed me off even more.

"Look, I don't know anything about this world. Not your pack, not your laws, and not you," I said, my voice rising. "You might share my DNA but you don't know me so you can't possibly be my family. You're just a girl who is standing in the way of me getting what I want."

"And what is that?" Regan asked, her voice dangerously soft.

"To go home. To pretend I never met a single one of you. Not even my father. If this is the world he lives in, I'll take my boring normal instead. And until someone recognizes that and sends me home, I'll be here. In this room. I won't compete. I won't play your little game. And you can't make me." It felt as if the day's events all seemed to pile on at once and the more I talked, the more certain I felt that I meant every word.

"You have to compete, Charlie," Regan said and it was all I could do to keep from attacking her. It was the only thing she could've said that would make this worse. "If you refuse, you'll forfeit."

"So what if I forfeit?" I demanded. "You can have it. Take the alpha spot. You seem much more prepared for it than I am."

"That may be," she said. "But this is it. There are no do-overs, no second chances. If you forfeit the competition, you forfeit the only chance you've ever had at belonging somewhere. More than that, at staying in the same place long enough to belong."

I opened my mouth to argue, but she cut me off. As heated as I'd been a moment ago, Regan was just as intent. "Don't try to deny you want that. I saw it on your face clear as day. You want to matter to people. You want roots. We are the only group that could ever possibly give that to you. And say what you want about Dad or me, but you care. I know you do. For better or worse, we're the only family you're going to get. Are you really prepared to forfeit that? To give it all up without a fight?"

I stared back at her until hot tears blurred her face. "I think fighting for it could be what costs me everything," I said quietly.

"What do you mean?" she asked.

I laughed, but it came out more like a cough. "Something tells me you aren't accustomed to second place."

My implication hung between us. As did her unspoken answer: she hadn't for a second considered I might beat her. I'd never felt less like a threat.

4

REGAN

My footsteps echoed against the rough planks of hardwood that led to Dad's office. I stopped outside the door and squared my shoulders. Footsteps startled me and I turned to find Carter coming up on my heels. His hair was windswept and my stomach flipped at the sight of the warmth in his eyes as he spotted me. Why did he have to look at me like that every time? And why did my body care? It was really annoying. I did not have time for this.

"Hey, boss," Carter said and I scowled.

"I'm not your boss," I said, careful to keep my voice low. I didn't want Dad overhearing this from the other side of the door.

"Not yet," he corrected. Still with the warm

blue eyes. Ocean eyes. Ugh.

"Didn't you hear Dad the other day?" I asked. "I'm not a shoo-in."

Carter looked at me like I'd spoken a foreign language. "Of course you are. A little competition never hurt anyone." Lines formed around his eyes as his gaze sharpened. "Wait. Are you actually worried your little sister might beat you?"

"No," I said on an exaggerated huff. I made a point to roll my eyes. "Shut up," I said before shoving the door open and walking inside.

Dad looked up from where he sat behind the desk, a tri-folded letter in his hands. He folded it along the creases and slid it away as we approached. I caught a glimpse of flowing handwriting before it disappeared underneath a stack of financial reports.

"Any news?" I asked, nodding at the papers.

"Hmm?" Dad glanced down at the pile. "Oh, no. These are personal. The investigation is still ongoing, though, don't worry."

I tried not to openly frown. "I can't help but worry, Dad. Those monsters snuck right into our town and murdered one of our own. We need to find out who did this and deal with them."

"We will," he assured me. "We're working on it, I promise you."

I sank into the chair in front of him, leaning forward, pleading. "If you'd just give me more details, I could help with—"

"Regan, your time as a leader is coming. I know you're antsy but try to enjoy the now. When all you have to worry about is today. Very soon, you will also be responsible for everyone else's tomorrow. It's not an easy thing."

I swallowed my response. Partly because he'd just made it sound like he assumed I'd be alpha. Or maybe he meant that even as second, I'd still be in charge. Either way, I knew better than to argue when Dad used that tone. As usual, Carter stood somewhere behind me. He, too, was quiet in the face of my dad's orders.

"How is she?" my dad asked, effectively changing—and closing out—the subject of my mother's killers.

I leaned back in the leather chair. "I wouldn't know. She still won't see me," I said.

Dad pressed his lips together; his thinking face. I braced myself for whatever order he was about to give. Chances were, when he wore that face, I wouldn't like it. "Carter, what about you?" Dad asked.

"She won't see anyone, sir. Barely taking her meals at this point," Carter said.

"What about her phone?" I asked. "Doesn't she still have the cell you gave her? Can we check for calls?"

"Already did," Dad said. "She hasn't made a single call. Not even her mother." I opened my mouth, but Dad cut me off and added, "I've already phoned her mother to assure her Charlie is safe."

A beat of silence passed and I wondered if Dad was finally going to admit he'd handled the situation wrong. He was still the only one of us who hadn't tried going to see Charlie. It didn't take a genius to see that he was the one she wanted to talk to.

But in the end, he straightened with a determined set to his face. “Regan, for better or worse, you are her sister. I know she’s in a bad place right now. We can’t imagine what with all these changes. But it’s up to you to reach her. To bring her into the pack. This is her home now, her family. We need to embrace her. And we need her to embrace us.”

“You might’ve thought of that before you dropped the whole ‘compete for your rightful place here’ bombshell on her,” I said and then because I couldn’t hold it in any longer, I added, “Why didn’t you tell me?”

Dad blinked at me, his blank expression almost worse than guilt. “I assumed you knew.”

“How would I know?” I snapped, and earned myself a glare. “Right. A good alpha knows everything about her pack, including its laws, however outdated,” I said, the sarcasm rolling off the words.

Dad opened his mouth but for once, I didn’t let him put me in my place for speaking out. “Got it,” I said, cutting him off.

I pushed to my feet and avoided Carter’s eye in case he was laughing at me. I focused instead on what the heck I was going to say to Charlie. Especially after I’d botched things so completely the last time we’d spoken. That was three days ago and she’d completely shut down after that. I still hadn’t told any of the others what we’d talked about. My own guilt was enough.

Dad’s next words stopped me in my tracks. “I could always send Sheridan to befriend her,” he said, his words far too light for the evil he'd just proposed.

I turned back to him, my emotions carefully in check. He was testing me, of that I was sure. And this time, I wasn't going to give him the satisfaction of seeing my displeasure. "You could also feed her to monkeys and watch them pick her apart bit by bit. I'll handle it," I said.

Dad chuckled. "Sheridan isn't that bad."

"She's not that good either," I said. This time, I didn't turn around as I left.

Carter caught up to me halfway to the woods. "Where are you going?" he asked, huffing at the effort it had taken to track me down.

I didn't slow or look away from my fixed point of the spruce half a mile into the trees. "To see a tree," I said.

"Any particular tree?" Carter asked wryly. "I mean, there's a bunch so…"

I spun so fast, he almost stumbled, and we both stopped. "Carter. I can't—" I stopped short, attempting to rein in the emotion I knew had crept into my expression. But it was too late. Too much to take back. Luckily, it was Carter. I could trust him. A good thing since the truth kept spilling out.

"This is a lot, all right? Dad gave me the one thing I've wanted all my life. My sister. And in the same breath, he took her away again. I'm supposed to befriend her and welcome her into the pack all the while plotting how I will defeat her. Dad would tell me the two aren't mutually exclusive. He'd tell me to stop feeling so much and just do what needs to be done. But … Look, in order to do that, I can't just joke it all away with you. I need…" I blew out a heavy breath. "That tree. It's quiet and has a low branch and I just want to sit. Okay?"

Carter didn't hesitate a single second as he nodded. "Okay. Let's go sit in a tree."

"You don't have to come with me," I said.

He waited and I knew he was testing to see if I'd refuse his offer outright. When I didn't, he brushed past me, headed for the woods. "I know," he said simply, already on his way so that I had no choice but to follow.

Sometimes, Carter's ability to manage me scared the crap out of me.

~5~

CHARLIE

My wolf was fighting claustrophobia.

I hadn't been outside in two days. I had no fingernails left to speak of and I could almost literally feel the Vitamin D in my bloodstream slowly leaking away. But after forty-eight hours of stubborn contemplation I still had no idea what to do.

Regan had been right. I wanted this. Or some better version of this. I loved my mom but I wanted family. The big, loud, annoying kind that got under your skin. The kind you always complained about but never really wanted to leave. I wanted a home. Roots. A place I belonged. And no matter how close my mom and I were, Oregon was never going to be that.

I still hadn't called her. By now, she was probably worried sick, so maybe it was self-preservation that kept me from dialing her. That and I knew she'd ask me what I wanted to do next. I had no clue.

The knock at the door jolted me and I felt myself flush at having jumped, even if no one was around to see it. "What?" I called in a curt voice to hide my embarrassment.

"Lunch," Brent said. Maybe it should've been comforting that he was always there, but Brent wasn't an endearing sort. In two days, we hadn't made it past "Lunch, dinner, and thanks." I wasn't holding out much hope for our future.

I went to the door and swung it open—and stopped short at the sight of my visitor. "You're not Brent."

"You're quick." Regan shoved my tray at me and stepped into the room before I could shut the door.

"What do you want?" I asked.

"I …" She stopped and when she answered, I knew she'd changed her mind against whatever she'd been about to say. "I want you to stay," she said finally.

Deep down, I knew those words were complicated truth. But right now, after two days of sitting in my own messy self-doubt and loneliness, I decided to accept them at face value. "I think … that's what I want too," I said.

She tried to smile, but it fell short. "I'm not going to pretend this isn't totally awkward but I do think you owe it to yourself to stick it out. So for what it's worth, I think you're making the right call."

The right call. So much love and warm fuzzies with this girl. I sighed. "And that's what you came up here to tell me?" I asked.

"Dad sent me up," she admitted. "He wants you to get a tour of the town."

"If I say no, are you going to hit me over the head and drag me there anyway?" I asked.

Her lips thinned and for a fraction of a second, I could see a real emotion pass over her face. Worry, or maybe concern, and then … nothing. Just as quickly as it had come, it left. In its place was even more control than had been there before. "I understand how hard this must be for you, finding out we all exist like this, but you don't really have a choice in being here."

Regan, the leader, the emotionless. I wanted to ask her how she did it, switching on and off like that, but I suspected that might ruin the semblance of civility we'd just established. "You might as well make the best of it," she added.

She had a point, though I wouldn't admit that out loud. Not to her. She was too sure of herself already. It made me feel ... small, somehow. I waited a beat to prove some point that probably didn't exist.

"Fine," I said. "Show me around."

Instead of turning to leave, she kept her feet planted and continued to stare at me.

"What?" I asked.

"I just ... You're shorter than I expected." She

looked like she wanted to say more, but she spun on her heel and exited the room. I hesitated, trying to decide if I'd just been insulted. Finally, still undecided, I followed her out.

I found her waiting in the hall. The same stocky guard from earlier eyed me like he suspected I'd run for it any second.

"That's enough, Brent. I got this." Regan gave him a stern nod and led me away. Brent stayed where he was, his eyes boring into my back all the way down the hall.

Regan led me down a flight of stained wood stairs and out the front door.

I tried to remember if I'd seen any of this on the way in, but I'd been so out of it—first from the knock on the head and then from some sort of drink they fed me during the drive—I barely remembered stumbling from the van into the house just before daylight.

But now, with a clear head and plenty of light, I saw how different the terrain looked from the town I'd left behind in Oregon. The front yard was long and narrow and cut off at the base of a steep hill. Farther below, I could see groupings of houses and buildings set in a wide circle. Beyond that, nothing but forest in every direction broken only by softly rolling hills that finally disappeared behind forest.

The air was warm and the sun was high in the sky. I wondered how long I'd been out, or exactly how far away from home I was.

"Pretty view," I said, leaving my voice flat against the compliment. I wasn't sure why I was being so difficult. This wasn't Regan's fault. But something about her reminded me so much of the man who called himself my father. And everyone else who'd lied. "Where are we?"

"Paradise," Regan said with a shrug.

I blinked at her. "Excuse me?"

"Paradise, California. The town was founded over one hundred years ago by the first wolf pack to travel from northern Canada into America. Current population seven hundred." She eyed me and hastily amended, "Seven hundred and one."

My eyed widened. "Wait. The town's population … all of them are like us?"

Regan laughed, a sharp, biting sound. "No. The pack totals about seventy, including small children and the council elders. Every one of them live in the group of houses you see below." She pointed to the houses clustered at the bottom of the hill. "We're just far enough outside of town to be considered our own village, if you will. Some of the elders have talked about going for our own township to cut ourselves off even more, but nothing's happened yet. So far, the humans pretty much leave us alone." She leaned over and lowered her voice to a whisper. "They think we're some sort of radical cult colony. If anyone asks, just say *Jesus Saves* in your craziest voice. They'll leave in you alone."

Any other day, it might've been funny. But after being kidnapped and meeting my estranged father and sister, nothing was funny about this situation. "Why are we up here?" I asked, gesturing to the house behind us.

"We are the alpha family, the most likely to be attacked. From down there, the pack has a clear view of the main house. They can see and protect us."

"Wouldn't living next door to the pack make it easier to defend us? So we're closer to help?" I asked.

"Being up here keeps the alpha separated from the commoners."

I stared at her, trying to figure out if she was serious. She didn't crack a smile, and I shook my head. Was my sister really that stuck up?

I followed Regan to the edge of the yard. When she kept walking past the garage, into the trees, I stopped. "I thought we were going to town."

"We are," she said.

"The car is parked back there." I pointed to the late-model Chevy truck parked on the side of the garage.

"We aren't taking the truck."

"Then how are we getting there?"

She looked at me like I was an idiot. "Running…"

She must've seen the surprise in my face because she walked back over to where I stood at the edge of the grass. She crossed her arms over her chest. "Is that a problem?" she added. There was no mistaking the challenge in her tone.

I met her gaze as steady as I could. "No problem."

She nodded once and then turned back to the forest. I followed and when she broke into a run, I increased my speed. I felt the wolf in me rise to the front of my mind, and I gave in. My bones cracked and shifted and, in mid-stride, furry paws extended out where my feet and arms had been. In the next step I landed on all fours, muscles rippling over furry shoulders. I sped up, gaining momentum and relaxing into my new body.

Regan was still a few steps ahead of me. Her wolf was a shade lighter than mine, its hair not quite as long. I stretched my neck side to side, straining the muscles of my jaw against the irritation my wolf felt at following instead of leading. That was a new feeling for me. I'd never run with anyone except my mother and she'd never felt this … bossy.

Regan increased the pace and my wolf matched it. Soon we were shoulder to shoulder. We sped down the hill, the greenery a blur around me. I was focused only on beating Regan. I didn't know where the town was and I didn't care. My wolf just wanted to win.

When Regan veered left, it took me a moment to notice and turn. By then, she was slowing and repositioning. Up ahead, I could see a small woodshed at the edge of a thick grove of trees. Beyond it, a house loomed on the other side of what looked like someone's backyard. A swing set stood, unused and rusted, on the sunburnt grass.

Regan steered us toward the house. I let her take the lead again, wary of a man-made building while still in this form. At the edge of the yard, Regan's wolf form shook around the edges. I could see her beginning to change. She stared me down, letting me know to do the same, and then squeezed her eyes shut as the change completed. When she was back on two legs, she stood and waited for me to join her.

I pushed the wolf to the back of my mind and pulled on the humanity underneath it. The fur shrank back and in its place were clothes, skin, fingernails. I shook my body, ridding it of the tingling that came from the change, and smoothed my hair. My sweatpants had returned and I was beginning to regret the choice in the heat of midday. California was a lot warmer than Oregon.

"You're pretty fast," Regan said.

My head came up. "Thanks." I had the feeling of being sized up. I shifted my weight, resisting the urge to fidget. "Ready?"

"Let's go." Regan led me through the side yard between two houses. The path emptied onto the circular street that encompassed the grouping of houses we stood between. Regan pointed at the house we'd passed. "That's Carter's house. His dad is the pack beta so he serves on the council."

"Is that like a board of directors or something?" I asked.

"Sort of. The council is made up of five families, including the alpha. They all get a vote in major pack decisions. Then there's the elder of elders. He gets two votes. He's the oldest living member of the pack and has been around since my great-grandparents ran things."

"And the beta position you keep talking about. What's that?"

"The alpha's right-hand man—or woman—is called the beta. It represents the second letter of the Greek alphabet and therefore symbolizes a second-in-command figurehead. Carter's dad was my mom's—" She swallowed. "Anyway, now he's my—our—dad's beta until a new alpha is named."

I wanted to reach out or say something meaningful, but words failed me. I didn't know this girl and something about her, while strong, felt so fragile. Like one wrong word would shatter … everything. So I ignored it in favor of our shared dilemma. "If our dad is alpha already, I don't understand why he can't just continue to be. At least for a while longer while we figure out this contest business."

Regan shook her head. "It's against pack law. The title must be passed to a female in the blood line. He's only temporary alpha by council vote. And even then it's only because of … what happened to my mom."

This time, I knew I couldn't ignore it. But before I could ask, she turned and cut across the street to the grassy courtyard in the middle of the cul-de-sac. I followed, glancing around. It dawned on me that things were very quiet here. Almost too quiet. No lawnmowers, no traffic, no mailman. Where was everybody?

Regan stopped in the center and faced the next house. "The houses here all belong to the council members. That one there is Sylvia Lantagne. She's older but super sweet and always knows when you're trying to sneak around. It's weird. And the one beside her is Judas Prescott." She rolled her eyes as she added, "He's never wrong." She turned again, moving clockwise. "And that last one there is Sheridan Waters." Regan shivered. "Don't piss her off. She's sort of scary. Like permanent PMS."

I smiled. "Noted."

"Seriously. Some freshman kid made the mistake of calling her out on an error she made on one of the recon reports and she made him run perimeter at the sewer plant for like six months. So gross." Regan wrinkled her nose.

"Patrols? You guys have a neighborhood watch or something?"

"We patrol twenty-four hours a day and everyone above the age of fifteen gets worked into the schedule. We have to be on our guard. Otherwise, well, look what happened to my mom." Her eyes flashed with grief fueled by anger.

"What did happen to your mom?" I asked quietly.

She stared into the trees and in a breathy voice said, "She was murdered."

"I'm sorry," I said. "Truly. I can't imagine…"

"My dad was out running patrols. I'd gone into town, to a movie with some friends." Her voice changed the longer she talked. It was touched with softness, and more than a little sadness, and I knew the wound was still fresh. "She was home alone and … the monsters got to her."

"So you know who did it?" I asked.

Her eyes flashed with anger, but she didn't get the chance to respond.

"Regan, hello." A woman with pin-straight blonde hair strode across the grassy courtyard toward us. A blue sports car idled in the driveway of the house behind her. I blinked. I hadn't even noticed her drive up.

"Sheridan." Regan nodded stiffly and instantly took on the calm and collected leader stance I'd seen her wear back at the house.

"Is this her?" Sheridan stuck her slender hand out toward me. "Charlotte, correct?"

I shook her hand and forced a smile. Even without Regan's warning there was something unlikeable about the woman. "It's Charlie. Nice to meet you."

"And you. We've all heard so much about you over the years." Her sharp eyes cut over my shoulder and back again within the spread of a heartbeat. "Did your mother accompany you?"

"No, she stayed behind," I said, wondering why she would ask me that if the pack had been the one to decide my mother wasn't welcome.

"Hmm." Her smile turned smug. "Better for her. We wouldn't want to add more of a load than she's already had to bear."

She tilted her head toward me and I could only assume the "load" she referred to was me. I had to bite my tongue against a sarcastic reply. Sheridan Waters, I decided, could go to hell.

"I was just showing Charlie around town," Regan said. I shot her a grateful look for changing the subject.

"Very good. I suspect I will see you both at the council meeting tomorrow evening. I trust Charlie will be … acclimated to her new situation by then." She eyed me like one would a child throwing a tantrum and then walked off. Her posture was ramrod straight and stiff.

"Geez, she walks like she has a stick up her—"

"Charlie," Regan hissed.

"She does."

"You can't say things like that about council members," Regan whispered as Sheridan headed for her car. She turned back once and waved before getting inside and driving off.

I shook my head. "But earlier, you said she had permanent—"

"I shouldn't have said that. It was disrespectful. An alpha always shows respect to the council and courtesy to the commoners." It sounded like a recitation, and I wondered if such statements would be part of my new "schooling" dear old Dad had mentioned.

"That sounds really stuck up," I said.

Regan looked at me sharply. "Let's keep moving."

We walked out of the cul-de-sac and down the street. At the stop sign a single car appeared from the other direction. It was the Chevy truck I'd seen at the house. One of the boys I'd seen, Carter I think, was driving. I tried to remember if he'd been one of my abductors but I couldn't be sure. He caught me watching and smiled and I decided then and there to like him anyway. His was the first genuine welcome I'd seen so far.

"You girls want a lift?" he asked.

"Thanks, Carter. We're fine." Regan's answer was short and clipped.

"You sure? It'd be a lot faster," he said.

Regan glared.

"Your dad said I should drive you," Carter added, clearly unbothered my Regan's coldness. He kept pace with us a moment more while Regan seemed to debate.

Eventually, Regan's shoulders sagged. "Fine," she agreed. "Charlie, get in."

She opened the door and stepped back so I was forced to slide in first. I wedged myself into the middle seat, one leg on each side of the gearshift, and tried to ignore the claustrophobia I felt at being crammed into such a small space.

As soon as Regan pulled the door shut Carter hit the gas and flipped a U-turn. We passed a few more houses on the way out of the neighborhood and I did see a few people out and about in the yard or getting into their cars. Carter turned out of the neighborhood and we picked up speed. It was a back road, winding and narrow, with the forest closing us in on both sides. In less than a mile it opened back up again and I could see a small strip of businesses and buildings up ahead. Carter slowed as we neared.

"So, this is it?" I asked, swiveling right and left to take it all in.

"Welcome to Paradise," Carter said with a wide arc of his arm.

Regan rolled her eyes. "This is town. Unless you want to drive twenty minutes into Hamilton City."

"Which we don't," Carter put in. "Not usually."

"On this side is the post office and the drugstore. On the left is the grocery and gas station," Regan said. She pointed to each as we passed even though they were clearly marked.

"What's that place?" I pointed to a broken-down building behind the drugstore.

"That's the movie theater. It's where I was

when Mom..." Regan trailed off.

No one said anything. Carter sped up and pointed out his window. "There's the high school."

"I thought Dad said I was going to be taught by the pack or him?" I asked.

"You are. I started homeschooling last year," said Regan. "All of the pack members are pulled junior year for homeschooling. It leaves more time for hunting and patrolling so the council makes it mandatory."

Up ahead, the stoplight changed and we rolled to a stop. "A blessing in disguise if you ask me. The humans there are a migraine waiting to happen," Carter said.

"That and you almost gave yourself away with that stupid flagpole prank last year," Regan said with an eye roll. She propped her elbow on the open window, casual and somehow at ease in the middle of their traded barbs.

"Not my fault," Carter protested. "They jumped me. Was I supposed to just stand there and take it?"

"Yes," Regan said, leaning forward a little as her intensity increased. I got the distinct impression these two argued a lot. "If it's a choice between showing off your superhuman strength and getting beat up, you get beat up."

Carter only smirked. "You're just jealous I took out all six of them without breaking a sweat."

"Anytime, anywhere, Carter, you just say the word," Regan said.

"My money's on her," I said, jerking a thumb at my new sister. I earned a laugh from them both.

The light changed and we passed the school

building, brick and brown trim and looking every bit as institutional as my own school back in Oregon. Up ahead, the road forked.

"Home?" Carter asked.

"Home," Regan agreed.

Carter took the road to the left and we sped up again. "What's the other way?" I asked. I strained my neck but the road wound around and disappeared out of sight. Regan and Carter exchanged a look.

"That's a story for later," Carter said. He sounded angry, though I couldn't figure out what had gone wrong except maybe Regan had promised me a tour of the town and all I'd gotten was a drive-by. But the air in the truck had thickened with something I didn't recognize, so I decided not to mention it.

We rode in silence for a few minutes. The road continued to wind and straighten and wind again as we slowly climbed higher toward the house on the hill. I hadn't realized we'd run so far earlier but I'd been distracted by the urge to compete.

"So have you figured out each other's strategy yet?" Carter asked.

"What do you mean?" I said.

"The contest. You're going to have to compete against each other." He glanced over at me. "You do realize that, right?"

"Yeah," I mumbled.

Regan didn't say anything. She had her lips pressed together and her arms folded again.

"I think it's ridiculous," he said.

I looked over at him. He was staring at the road

and shaking his head in disgust. "Our competition?" I asked, hoping I'd finally found an ally to talk them all out of it.

"The loser gets to be beta," he said.

"Sad you're losing your place?" Regan asked him.

"It's rightfully mine. I should get a say," he said.

"No, it's rightfully the alpha's choice," she shot back.

"We both know—" His cheeks reddened and he stopped. "I shouldn't have to lose it to a newbie," he finished. They exchanged a glare over my head and I wished I could've sunk into the seat.

No one said anything else after that.

At the top of the hill I spotted two large utility vans that hadn't been there earlier parked in front of the garage.

"What's going on?" I asked.

Neither of them answered. I stole a glance at each of them, but they looked just as stumped as I was. We got out and Carter wandered off. I stayed with Regan because even though I didn't exactly get a warm fuzzy around her, she was the closest thing to a friend I had made so far. I followed her around the side of the house. Workers in gray uniforms were carrying tables and chairs down a wide path that led straight into the woods.

"What the hell...?" Regan mumbled.

We fell into step side by side and a few minutes later the path opened into a wide clearing. Thick trees bordered all sides, but under my feet was thick grass. I looked down and realized it wasn't even natural; it was some kind of fancy AstroTurf. The space was clearly being prepared for a party.

Fairy lights were draped from the branches of the trees that hung over the open area while long benches carved out of tree trunks were dragged into position on either side of a wide aisle. A couple of muscled men were ripping pine trees out of the ground where they came too close to the clearing and throwing them aside. They gave loud cracking noises as the roots were wrenched free of the earth. I flinched every time, more in awe of their show of brute force than the violent noise of the dying trees. I'd known my whole life we possessed strength like this—I'd never actually tested the limits. Or watched others do the same.

"Hello, girls." William Vuk walked up, nodding politely in the way a dinner guest might. He stood with his hand at his sides and his chest out, the picture of confidence and power. He was watching the work with a keen eye that said he didn't miss a single detail. None of it was familiar or even affectionate. I noticed Regan was just as detached in the way she stood half-facing us, half-ready to bolt.

"Dad, what's going on?" Regan asked.

"We're getting ready for a wedding," he said, the words so matter-of-fact, I was surprised Regan didn't already know. It felt like everyone knew what was going on but me.

"It looks like a pretty big deal," I said. "Who's going to be married?"

"You are," he said. And then, turning to Regan, added, "Or maybe it will be you."

I felt all the blood rush out of my head. The world spun around me, and I had to grab one of the benches to stay standing. “Excuse me? I’m … You’re joking. This is a joke, right?”

Regan was pale and deathly silent beside me.

“Not a joke,” he corrected. “Rather a pledge. Tonight, we are hosting an engagement party for the impending marriage of the next alpha. Whichever of my daughters that turns out to be.”

My half-sister stiffened behind him. Her eyes went round and her nostrils flared.

“That doesn’t make any sense,” I protested.

“It makes too much sense, and there’s the logic in it that can’t be overlooked, unfortunately. No matter our ... feelings,” he said with a pointed look at Regan that sent a ripple of dread through me.

“Dad, what did you do?” Regan asked.

“It’s time for both of you to learn about the treaty,” Dad said. “Sit down.”

I did what he told me to, but not because I wanted to be obedient. I just didn’t have any other choice. My legs wouldn’t hold me up anymore. Regan didn’t budge, but she was breathing hard, and I guessed she hadn’t known any more about the marriage thing than I did.

Marriage? Was he crazy? Had living out here in isolation amongst only werewolves rotted his brain?

“Look, whatever you’re trying to do, traditions to uphold and all that, it’s not for me. I can’t get married,” I said, trying to sound as calm as possible while my brain whirled in hysteric circles. “I’m not old enough. I’m not in love. I’m not—”

"An organization as old and noble as our pack has enemies," my dad began as if I hadn't even spoken. "This shouldn't come as a surprise to you. But in this modern day, we can't openly wage war anymore. If we spill blood across the forest in the heat of battle, humans will notice, and there could be ... problems." Dad kind of looked wistful about that, like he thought it was a shame he couldn't maul his enemies. "We've been forced to find better ways to resolve disputes. Negotiations, politics, acts of good faith toward peace." He said the last word with distaste.

"What does this have to do with a wedding?" I asked.

"The Council of Elders and I have been working to arrange a marriage that benefits all parties. This goes back to before your mother was killed, Regan," he warned. "This is the best way."

"All parties? What does that even mean?" I demanded. All his talk of wars and elders and disputes was making my head spin.

"It means whichever daughter assumes the role of alpha will wed Owen Rossi."

My exclamation was drowned out by a resounding, "Hell no," from Regan. I wasn't sure who this Owen person was, but he must be pretty horrible. It was the first time I'd heard her disagree with anything Dad said, but as soon as the words were out of her mouth her face reddened and she dropped her eyes. "Sorry, sir. But I mean, isn't that a bad idea? No, a horrible, wretched, unthinkable idea? They killed Mom."

"We don't know who killed her, Regan, and

that's what I intend to find out." Dad looked back at the wedding preparations like a drill sergeant inspecting a bunker. "One way or another," he muttered. "But that's not your concern. A marriage between our families will bring goodwill and peace at a time the pack needs it most." He frowned. "This is purely political. You don't have to like it. You just have to do it."

I looked at Regan, hoping she'd say something, anything, to convince our dad he was being crazy. I couldn't be expected to marry a complete stranger, especially one so horrible Regan suspected him of murder. Who was this guy? Another werewolf, I assumed. But Regan wasn't giving up anything; she'd recovered from her earlier outburst and was tensely silent. She met my gaze and I could see the burn of temper underneath the surface, but she didn't speak. I was on my own.

"You can't expect me to be a part of whatever political game you're playing," I said. "This is stupid!"

Dad gripped my shoulder. His hand was heavy and it clenched down tight on my clavicle, but not painfully so. His glare hurt more. It sliced right through me.

"I expect you to do what you must to save the lives of the pack. You are a Vuk. I expect you to act like it." He included Regan in his glance. She stared back for a half a second before her gaze fell away. I could understand that; Dad wasn't the type you could stare down.

My silence must've satisfied him because he let go of me and stepped back, eyeing the progress of the workers again.

"Hey, that doesn't go there," he snapped at a harried-looking boy with glasses.

The boy was balancing a stack of chairs in his arms and they were wobbling side to side while he tried to figure out where Dad was pointing. "I'll see you both at the meeting later," he said, barely glancing at us as he strode toward the now frightened-looking boy.

I turned back to Regan. She was standing rod straight and staring hard after Dad. "How bad is it?" I asked. She blinked, almost like she'd forgotten I was there. "This wedding," I prompted when she didn't answer. "Owen what's-his-name."

"Rossi," she muttered. "It's beyond ridiculous. That's what it is."

"Did he really kill your mother?"

"Well, not him personally. I mean, he could've but I doubt he'd get his hands dirty with mercenary work. He'd send someone. That bodyguard of theirs is high on my list."

"He has a bodyguard?" Her explanation was getting more and more confusing. Who was this guy? If his family was so powerful around here, how come no one had mentioned him on our tour of the town? Maybe he was from a different pack farther away.

"His whole family does." She smirked. "They just don't want me to catch them alone."

I thought of the men yanking trees out with their bare hands. Of Carter fighting off six human kids at school without breaking a sweat. I could only imagine what Regan was capable of in a fight.

"What did they do to make everyone hate them so much?"

She rolled her eyes, like the answer should've been obvious. "They don't have to do anything. It's what they are."

I shook my head, thoroughly confused. "Which is?"

"Hey, Vuk," someone called from the other end of the field.

Both Regan and I turned and I immediately felt my cheeks flush at reacting to the name. Carter was coming toward us, and he was clearly talking to Regan. Why would anyone here be calling out to me? "Bevin just called. She said to tell you she'll meet you at the training field tomorrow at seven," he told her.

"Thanks," Regan said.

Carter's brow quirked. "What's that about?"

"What do you mean?" she asked.

"You meeting my sister at the ungodly hour of seven in the morning."

"Oh." Regan shot me a glance and I got the feeling I was suddenly unwanted. I looked around, but it wasn't like there was anywhere for me to go. "She's going to help me get some training time in. For the competition," she said, shooting me another glance.

Light dawned on Carter's face. "Gotcha."

I kept my gaze averted, like I hadn't just heard all of that, but it was insanely awkward. So Regan was already setting aside time to practice to beat me in the competition? Clearly, she'd already bought into the whole duel idea our father had planted. Was

I the only one who thought this was crazy? Or outdated?

"So, what's the deal with your old man, anyway?" Carter asked. "I just heard about the Rossi thing. This wedding idea is bullshit. Even he has to know that."

"You would think." Regan shook her head. I followed her line of sight to where Dad was still berating the kid with the chairs and making sure he placed every single one of them perfectly. "I don't know. He seems to think they're innocent and that we should unite our families to end the feud. Blah, blah, blah."

Carter's brows furrowed in what looked like genuine concern. "You think losing your mom pushed him over the edge?"

"I don't know. Doesn't matter. He says the Council agrees with him, and it's not like we could argue anyway. Don't forget he's the acting alpha right now."

Carter scowled. "How could I forget? But seriously, marrying Rossi? That's just insane. What are you going to do?"

"I'll figure something out," Regan muttered.

Carter continued to talk to Regan about names and events I'd never heard of. I tuned it out and tried to think of a good reason to excuse myself. I was dying for a reason to leave and they both spoke like I wasn't there anyway. I couldn't believe Regan was going to train the next day. Had the entire day—all of our time spent getting to know each other—been a lie? Did she even want to know me? Or was she just trying to get information from me, to find out how to take me down? I'd had enough.

"I'm going back to my room," I said, abruptly cutting off whatever Carter was saying about patrol schedules and the party security. Both of them just looked at me like they'd forgotten I was there.

"Give me a second, I'll go with you," Regan began.

"I can find my own way," I said, cutting her off. I turned and walked off, leaving her and Carter to discuss my demise in private.

~6~

REGAN

My wolf muscles burned and screamed, protesting against the strain, but I didn't let up. In front of me, my friend Bevin was a furry outline with pointed teeth. The gray dawn mixed with the soft gray in her fur—Carter always teased it ended up that shade from dying her human hair too often—until the only thing I could make out were her black eyes and her razor canines. Both of us were panting heavily. Bevin's mouth hung open just enough and I knew if her jaw found purchase against any part of my wolf, she wouldn't hesitate to bite.

Neither would I.

That's what I liked about Bevin. She never went easy. As a wolf, at least. As a human teenaged girl, she sometimes got too dramatic for me. But like this, we were a good match for me to let off some steam.

I growled as I blocked Bevin's next attack, forcing myself to refocus. Part of me was too cocky to admit I needed the practice, especially against someone like Charlie. But there was a small voice way down deep that wondered…

"You're distracted," Bevin said a few minutes later when I'd managed to block her but not launch any successful attack of my own.

She backed away and began to shudder at the edges of her form. I did the same, managing to concentrate long enough to be certain my clothes stayed with me as I shifted back to two legs. Bevin shook her head.

"You better get it together before the contest," she said.

"Don't remind me," I muttered.

"Some of the pack are saying your dad has lost it," she admitted.

"They might be right." I sighed and swiped my hand over my face. "It doesn't make any sense. The Rossis have to be behind Mom's—it doesn't make any sense," I repeated.

Bevin didn't reply.

There was nothing to say. As crazy as it was, we both knew I didn't have a choice in any of it. Pack law had spoken.

We stood apart and stretched in silence. My mind wandered to Charlie. To the way she'd stalked off yesterday. Guilt tugged at me for the way Carter and I had argued in front of her. After all the progress we'd made with that little trip into town and then we'd ruined it with our bickering. But did he have to mention my training time with Bev right in front of her? I shook my head as I reached for my toes and felt the pull behind my knees. Sometimes, Carter didn't think it through.

Even after we were finished, Bevin stayed unnaturally quiet. I glanced over at her as we gathered our things but she didn't notice. Her subtle muscles pulled as she hoisted a couple of weights back into her duffel. We'd used them earlier during some resistance exercises. I hated that part but Bev loved them and I knew her enthusiasm would push me. I hadn't been wrong, but I was sure as hell going to be stiff tomorrow.

Bevin finished packing up and hovered nearby, biting her lip. I knew there must be something on her mind, though I didn't press it. She'd get there.

"Carter's in a weird funk," she said finally.

"I bet he is," I said, grabbing a towel from the bag I'd brought with me and patting my face. Even this early, there was still enough heat forming to have worked up a sweat. "Sucks knowing he's lost his spot," I added, because I knew as his sister, Bevin was probably bummed too.

"I don't think it's that," she said.

"The Rossi thing?" I asked, frowning. I still couldn't believe Dad had made a deal with those monsters.

"Yes, I think so," she admitted. "But it's not …"

I reached for a couple of waters and tossed one over. She caught it easily but only fiddled with it absently. My impatience got the better of me and I rolled my eyes.

"Spit it out, Bev. What's up?" I asked.

Bevin's eyes darted to mine and when they held there, their dark-blue depths reminded me so much of Carter, I had to step back. There was the warmth of friendship I wasn't accustomed to with my own family but it came with such a deep streak of loyalty that burned hot against the early morning, I wondered how I'd never seen it before. Maybe I'd never had a reason.

Her muscled arms moved the cap to the water bottle until it twisted freely. Still, she only cupped it without lifting it to her lips. Her angular face was tight with tension and I watched as her jaw muscle worked while her mind searched for words.

"He won't let you marry Rossi—if it comes to that," she said finally.

"What do you mean he 'won't let me?'" I repeated, a twinge of something strange lacing my gut. "It's not up to Carter. He's not beta—"

"It's not about beta," Bevin huffed. "It's about *you*, Regan. You don't even see—" She threw up her hand and instead of finishing the statement, she tossed back the contents of the bottle, chugging until it was empty.

Still, I stood in confusion.

Bevin tossed the bottle into my open bag and swiped at her mouth with a suntanned arm. She stepped closer until we stood eye to eye. Our height had always been perfectly matched, with Bevin's shoulders and hips just a little wider than mine. Seventeen years of tight friendship seemed to pass between us and then the heat flared again.

"I won't let you lose," she said fiercely. "No matter what, you will lead. But Carter … it will hurt him if you marry Rossi. I can't stop that. I can't help it. You're my alpha, Regan. But you're also my friend. So I'm telling you this. If Carter finds out, he'll skin me, but there it is. Do what you want with it."

She spun on her heel, snatched her own bag from the field, and retreated toward the woods that bordered home. I watched her go, still sifting through her words, trying to decipher their meaning. What did it matter to Carter who I married? All he wanted was to be beta. Probably so he could argue with me every day until it killed us.

And what the heck was up with Bevin's crazy-eyed promise of my victory? It sounded an awful lot like a threat. And the weird part was I didn't like the idea of anyone threatening my little sister.

~7~

CHARLIE

I hadn't meant to sleep, but when I opened my eyes the light through the window was pre-dawn gray. I whipped the covers aside and hurried over for a closer look. Nothing moved in the yard below me. It was hard to see if the coast was clear with my weak human eyes.

I needed to get out of the house.

Somewhere between getting shown around the little hole of a town and being told I was semi-betrothed to some guy I'd never met, I had made a decision: daughter of the alpha or not, I was not going to put up with some crazy werewolf pack running my life.

I was leaving, and there was nothing they could

say to stop me. If they found me and dragged me back a hundred times, I'd leave a hundred and one. Maybe, eventually, they'd get sick of it and just leave me be.

I dressed quickly, as quietly as I could in the still house. Every creak underneath my feet felt like an alarm, but no one came. At the door, I hesitated. The tiny cell phone was a pulsing temptation on my nightstand, but in the end, I left it behind. Mom would be worried, but I couldn't go back there. Not right away. It's the first place they'd check, starting with the phone records for this little number they'd so graciously provided. I was new to pack life, not born yesterday.

I eased my bedroom door open, fully expecting Brent to be standing there glaring at me. But the hall was empty. Apparently, they'd graduated me to "trustworthy at night."

I held my breath the entire way downstairs, so sure someone was going to snatch me from behind or block my path. But as I tore across the backyard and into the thick woods beyond, my inner wolf rising to the surface, the feeling of freedom was unmistakable.

I'd made it. I was getting out.

I ran all-out for three miles before I stopped to breathe. By then, even my wolf was exhausted and breathless. My sides heaved as my animal lungs gasped for air. It was only a matter of time before they realized I was gone. I could really only allow short breaks like this before resuming my journey north. I had to get out of the forest before they caught my scent or it was over.

I hadn't even meant to go this way, but like a magnet drawn to its other half, my heart was leading me to Oregon. Maybe I could call my mom and have her meet me. We could run together. Settle in the next destination. Resume our life somewhere else, like we'd always done.

I started running again, deeper into the dark growth. The trees were closer together and didn't let the first hints of sunlight reach the ground, especially now, when the horizon was only beginning to catch a hint of the coming day. Shadows hunched in shadows. I caught a strange scent just ahead and faltered.

It was like nothing I'd ever smelled before. The smell was sickly sweet, reminding me of a dead animal in the woods that hadn't begun to rot. But something else mixed with it. Something unique and alluring in its strangeness. I wandered closer, both wary and curious.

Leaves parted and the path up ahead broke open, giving me a full view. With my animal's sharpened senses, it took only seconds to spot the source.

There, standing in the cradle of a fallen tree, was a person. He was definitely male, solid without appearing overly muscular. I sniffed. Not a werewolf but … not quite human either. My nose twitched at that even as my brain rejected it. Those were the only two choices—it didn't make sense.

He stood on the broken log of an ancient oak and leaned against another tree, breaking branches with his hands. He snapped another twig and his lip curled, like he was disgusted by it somehow. I padded closer, the curious animal in me drawn to this strange specimen. He smelled strange; exotic and dangerous. There was something about him...

I crept closer, trying to get a better look at him. Even from here, the strong line of his jaw was tense and through his tee I saw that his shoulders were rigid with stress. He moved quickly from branch to snapped branch—faster than any other human I'd seen. And precise, as if despite the speed, every movement was measured and calculated down to the second.

As he moved, my attention caught not on his impossible speed, but on his face. Strong, silent, and masculine—except for the thick lashes that framed sharp, piercing irises.

My wolf muscles contracted automatically at the sight of them. *Predator,* every nerve in me screamed. I shook it away—that was crazy. He was a *person*.

As if I'd called the words aloud, his eyes snapped up, searching and scanning the undergrowth. I held my breath and froze. The hair on the sides of my neck rose in panic. How had he heard my silent footsteps? No human could have heard that.

His eyes tracked over the trees and settled on the very spot I was crouched in. His gaze seemed to lock onto mine, despite the distance and brush cover that separated us. The animal in me spooked; the desire to flee was overwhelming. But something made me hesitate.

One second was all it took.

He was on me faster than a blink. Arms

extended in a full-body tackle, we went down and rolled across the forest floor. My snarls mixed with his grunts as we both struggled for the upper hand. I'd never actually fought someone before, let alone in my wolf form. I'd wrestled around a little with my mother as a pup, but nothing like this. It was terrifying. I wasn't sure how long I could go without actually hurting him. Despite his amazing speed and accuracy, he was still a person. And I was a wolf.

But even as I thought it, the strange sweet smell from earlier grew thicker around me until it filled my nostrils and drove out everything else. My wolf wanted to kill whatever was attached to that smell. The human in me was horrified.

He tried driving his fist into my shoulder, but I dodged him and jumped back as I scrambled to my feet.

I circled him, wary of his speed and the deadly look in his eyes. He didn't look nearly as afraid as I thought he should. He looked ... vicious. Up close, his hair was darker than mine and long enough to fall just short of his brow. It contrasted sharply with his fair skin, like someone who didn't spend much time outside. And his eyes—those were the worst. I found it hard to look away, especially with him staring at me so intently, but there was a violence underneath his calm intensity that made me think twice about his slight build.

Something in him wanted to hurt me just as badly as I did him.

He came at me again and I dodged, crouching into a low, threatening stance. I pulled my lips back from my teeth and growled in what I hoped was a menacing sound. Instead of turning and running, he just planted his feet and narrowed his eyes. His jaw was set like he was more determined than ever.

"Come on, then. Screw a truce. You want to take me down, don't you?"

The sound of his voice was unexpected, maybe because I couldn't summon the use of mine in my own shock and panic of our fight. It startled me, and he saw his opening. He lunged and his arms found their way around me. His hands clasped my neck and squeezed. Within seconds, my windpipe began to close underneath the pressure. I heard myself yelp before it morphed into something like a whimper.

"Not so scary without your pack, are you?" he demanded in a crooning voice that left no doubt he'd killed before—and that he intended to do it again now. "It would've taken a lot more than one of you to take me down. You should've stuck with your friends."

I tried to yelp, call out, anything to make him let up on the pressure around my neck. But I couldn't breathe, much less talk. I couldn't even think. He obviously thought I was part of the pack and had decided to even some score he had with them. I didn't have a way to convince him I wasn't.

Suddenly it didn't matter what he was—human, wolf, or otherwise—this was it. He was nothing more than my murderer.

His pressure increased and I knew there wasn't a thing I could do to stop it. Well, there was one thing I could do, but if I was wrong, it would only speed up my death. I was starting to feel light-headed and I knew I didn't have much time no matter what I chose, so did the only thing left.

I shifted.

My attacker's eyes widened as, slower than usual under the physical strain, my human form returned. When my limbs had separated into two arms and two legs, and flesh replaced fur, I felt his grip loosen as my throat slimmed to the breadth of a girl instead of a wolf. I sucked in a ragged breath, desperate to recover before he could compensate for the difference and choke me again.

"What the...?" He jerked his hands away and I rolled away, gasping and jerking as oxygen struggled to return to my lungs. I couldn't even get off my hands and knees.

I was hacking and coughing into the dirt, my eyes watering, when a blurred hand appeared in front of me.

I blinked to clear my vision before I allowed my gaze to travel up his arm to his face. He looked different now that I had human eyes. Instead of simply pale, his skin was radiant in its translucence. Beautiful, really. He was tall and slender and brooding, with those same piercing eyes. Only now, they were mesmerizing, drawing me in. Inviting me to uncover the secrets held deep inside them. They widened, his lashes spreading and lifting as he stared back at me, full lips parted in surprise. He looked just as stunned to see me as I was to see him.

I tensed, half-expecting him to use his still-extended hand to attack me again. But he didn't.

Strange as it was, there was something in that

handsome face that made me relax despite the violence a moment ago. Maybe it was the way his parted lips softened the jagged lines of his jaw and cheekbones, or the way his hair curled gently over his ears, but there was something gentle underneath the cold demeanor.

Against all logic, I trusted him.

"Thanks," I managed, finally taking his hand and allowing him to pull me to my feet. His skin was cool, but it felt good after the heat of the fight. He let out a short laugh and I looked up at him as I straightened, self-conscious about how disheveled I must be. "What?" I asked, warily. Even after the single word, my throat ached. It would probably keep hurting until I healed it by shifting again. But I'd stay human if it meant he backed off and stopped trying to kill me.

"I just finished trying to kill you and you're thanking me?" he asked, brows raised in a perfect arch.

"Not for the almost killing part," I said. "But for the helping me up part. Or for not killing me."

"Well, which is it?" he asked, brows still arched, but now it seemed more of a challenge.

"Take your pick," I said with a shrug that said I couldn't care less.

His lips curved in amusement. "You're not part of the pack," he said.

"Does that mean you're not going to try and kill me again?" I asked.

His eyes crinkled in a smile, forming tiny lines at the edges that only served to make him hotter. "Only if you promise the same restraint," he said.

"Deal." I eyed him, still wary but relieved.

Farther out, a bird called and I jumped. Subtle, but I could see that he noticed. He kept his distance even as his expression softened. "What are you doing out here, little wolf? Far from home, I take it."

I hesitated. I couldn't tell him the truth. He obviously knew the pack. The last thing I needed was him mentioning that he'd seen me here.

"Running," I said, shrugging like it was no big deal.

"Running," he repeated. He quirked a brow at me, clearly unimpressed. The gesture, the way it highlighted his warm eyes and thick lashes, made my heart pump faster.

"What are you doing out here?" I countered, making my tone as rude as possible to cover my nerves.

"Same as you," he said. And after a brief hesitation of his own, added, "Escaping."

I wanted to ask him from what but then I'd have to tell him my own issues. I wasn't ready for that quite yet so I asked the next question. "What the hell are you, anyway? I've never seen someone fight like you."

"You've never seen someone..." He trailed off, staring at me with even wider eyes than before. "Do you mean…?"

"Do I mean what?" I asked. He didn't answer, only watched me in something like suspicion. "Well? Are you going to answer me?"

"You either don't know or … But you must know. You've got to be joking. This is a prank.

Who sent you? Is your pack watching this? Is that Regan watching right now?" He turned in circles, peering into the forest around us.

"No one's watching." *I hope*, I added silently. I didn't want to think of how the pack would react to seeing their possible future alpha's ass getting kicked.

I folded my arms across my chest, attempting to look like I meant business. Mostly because the way he was looking at me was making my heart race pulse at ridiculous speeds—even my wolf pulse wasn't this high. Ridiculous, I told myself. No boy had ever affected me this way. Not that he was a boy. Clearly he was something else. "I'm being serious," I added, hoping I sounded convincing. "I know you're … something other. What are you?"

He turned back to me and when I blinked again, he was standing a foot away from me. I jumped back and he grinned. His canines were lengthened into fine points, almost like mine when I was a wolf, but more slender. Like the fangs of a snake. His breath hit my cheek in puffs of sweet air.

"I'm a vampire," he breathed.

A vampire.

Nothing should have surprised me after everything else I had been through. I mean, I was a teen werewolf, who had grown up with a werewolf mom, and I had been kidnapped by a whole pack of werewolves. There was nothing normal about growing fur and a tail whenever I wanted. So if we existed, didn't it make sense that other supernaturals would, too?

But I always imagined vampires being

something creepy and slimy lurking in a castle, like Dracula with his big cape and the overblown Transylvanian accent. This guy was nothing like that. He looked strong, but slender, and when he spoke it felt as though I was being caressed with his silken voice. His eyes smoldered with dark fire that was both alluring and deadly all at once.

If he had said he was a model or an actor, I would have believed him. Or even a hypnotist or snake charmer or some other trained magician. But a vampire?

On the other hand, the fangs were pretty convincing.

"Oh," I said finally. It probably sounded just as stupid as it felt to say it, but my brain wasn't capable of producing anything better at the moment.

He laughed. It was a wonderful, rich sound, and I found myself unconsciously leaning toward him. "You really had no idea," he said softly, shaking his head, and then almost to himself he added, "You're very unexpected."

"I mean, you're not what I thought a vampire would look like," I said, trying—and failing again—to come up with some quick-witted response. But my brain felt stuck on processing the word he'd given me. Vampire. Is that why my wolf wanted to attack him? Were we natural enemies or something?

"I do hope that's a compliment," he said.

I felt my cheeks heat and let my answer drop. "I didn't know vampires were real. That sounds silly but I guess I thought … Shifters, wolves, were the only supernatural thing out there."

"Lucky for you, you were wrong," he said and I didn't miss the note of teasing. Or flirting.

Was he flirting with me? I forced my attention back to the conversation before my clammy palms could begin sweating at the thought.

"Vampires are … I mean, you drink blood and all that?" I asked, earning a laugh.

I took that as my answer but from there, the questions flooded in as acceptance dawned. Vampires were real. But what were the rules? Did he age normally? Was he a thousand years old? How strong was he? Judging by the ache in my throat, I had a good idea. I opened my mouth to ask one or more of these questions, but he held up his hand, clucking. "I've answered one of yours. Now you get to answer one of mine."

I frowned. "Fine," I said.

"My precious little runner, tell me this—are you running toward something or away?"

I could have lied. It would have been easy, and, in fact, it would have been safer for me. When I opened my mouth, I fully intended to say that I was just having fun. Out for a jog.

Instead, my gaze locked on his and the truth came tumbling out.

"I had to get away. That pack—they're crazy." I lowered my voice. "They kill things."

"And you don't?" he asked, a smirk ghosting his lips.

"No," I said, "of course not."

His smile disappeared and eyes widened the smallest sliver. Was he surprised by my announcement or my naiveté?

He stepped closer to me, circling and giving me a long, up-and-down look from feet to head that made me feel a little dirty. Like he was imagining me naked. "You aren't what I would have expected at all," he murmured.

His breath was cool on my neck. I tried to hide my shiver.

"Who are you?" I asked, my back prickling at the way he seemed to draw me to him without even trying.

"Who am I? That's an excellent question." He gave me a closed-lipped smile. The points of his fangs left little indents in his bottom lip. "Who am I? Hmm."

I straightened my shoulders and focused on the point of his nose rather than meeting his gaze directly. It was slightly easier this way to maintain my wits. "It's not a difficult question."

"Not a simple answer, either. And even if I answered your question, it wouldn't tell you what you wanted to know," he said.

I rolled my eyes. "Are you always this cryptic?"

"Are you always such a coward?" he shot back.

"I'm not a coward!" If I'd still had my fur, it would've risen on end at his comment. I felt guilty of his accusation even though I knew I shouldn't, and became immediately defensive. "I don't belong here."

"And why is that?" he asked, head cocked.

I tried to put it into words without giving too much away. I still wasn't sure I should be talking to him. He'd made it clear he wasn't friends with the pack. But something about him made it impossible for me to ignore his barbs and questions. He watched me and waited as if he truly wanted to know the answers. As if he wanted to understand me. It was more than I could say for any of them. "Sharing blood with people doesn't make you the same as them," I said carefully.

His eyes flickered with understanding and I realized too late that I'd just admitted to being related to one of them. I held my breath, waiting to see if the realization changed things. Maybe he'd attack me again after all. But he didn't move toward me.

"Can't disagree with you there, darling, but is it so bad that you need to flee?" he asked. Still casual, as if the admission didn't mean anything to him.

My shoulders slumped. I'd come this far, might as well lay it all out. "I'm being forced to fight my sister," I said. "For the role of alpha."

His eyes flickered with sudden interest that burned as he stared back at me. I looked away, too drawn in to risk looking at him now. "I see," he said quietly. "I take it you're new to their group. Seems counter-intuitive to building a familial bond throwing you to the wolves." Hips lips twitched. "Pardon the pun."

"How do you know I'm new?" I asked.

"Because, darling, I would've remembered you. Trust me," he said and my heart pattered irregularly. I frowned, forcing myself to focus. This was not normal, wanting to kill a guy and then wanting to kiss him all in the space of minutes. Maybe the stress was getting to me. Maybe I was desperate to cling to anyone who would listen.

Or maybe this guy could help me somehow. He clearly had knowledge of the pack. Maybe he could find a way to help me out of this mess.

"The alpha role is apparently only passed to the females in the line," I explained. "Some sort of law or tradition. My father—whom I just met yesterday—insists my sister and I compete against each other. Some sort of fight for the title. How can they expect me to fight my own sister? Especially when I know nothing about these people. She's been here her entire life, while I've been stuck in human-ville. I have no chance of winning and after meeting them, I realize no chance at ever being close either." I sighed. "Unless I can find a way to stop this, I think it's best if I just go."

"You speak of Regan Vuk?" he asked. "You're her sister?"

"Half-sisters, apparently." I wandered back over to him, suddenly aware that I'd been pacing—and that I'd just basically unloaded my entire situation onto this stranger, for no reason other than that he seemed trustworthy in a way that wasn't definable by words.

"Half-sisters. How intriguing," he murmured. His gaze sharpened. "And you think running away will solve your problem? That they won't come after you and force you to do this?"

My shoulders slumped. "No. I don't know."

"If there were any chance for a familial bond with them, would you stay?" he asked.

"Of course. I mean, aside from this crazy battle and … the other stuff," I said, realizing the arranged marriage was a whole other can of worms. One I didn't want to explain just yet. "I'd love to have a sister. A dad. You know, people like me."

"We all need to understand our roots," he said, nodding. "Where we come from is just as important as where we're going."

"Even if those roots are twisted up in outdated traditions and laws designed to limit your choices rather than expand them?" I challenged.

"No one said progress was easy," he said, and something in his words made it seem more personal than some repeated cliché.

"What am I supposed to do?" I asked.

"That," he said, his lips curving slightly, "is not something I should answer for you. But I think you already know."

His eyes flickered to something behind us and we both tensed. A second later, a small rustling sound reached my ears.

Crap, the pack.

I whirled back to mystery guy.

"Looks like our time is up," he said, and there was a note of regret in his words that made me flush. He was shifting his weight from side to side, and I could see that he was ready to bolt, but something made him pause.

"Wait," I said, extending my hand toward him. I'm not sure why. It's not like I was strong enough to hold him in place against his will—our fight had proven that. "You didn't tell me your name."

He turned back long enough to reach up and tuck a runaway strand of my hair behind my ear. His fingers were feather light against my cheek, but the tingling trail they left behind caused my breath to hitch. "Another time," he murmured close enough that his warm breath washed over me in a sweet cloud.

I blinked, inhaling. And then he was gone, with nothing but a swirl of leaves where his feet had stood to mark his presence.

The distant rustling grew louder, closer. I grimaced.

The vampire was right. Running away wasn't going to solve this. I had to face it, one way or another. But I wasn't going to do it while admitting I'd been roaming out here alone. Fighting off vampires. And I needed to heal my aching throat.

I called my wolf up and shifted just as the first werewolf appeared through the trees.

The tawny wolf growled when it spotted me. I growled back, determined not to be intimidated. Another wolf appeared, bigger and bulkier than the first. His fur was mud-brown and coarse, like he didn't worry much about grooming. He, too, growled and glared at me. They advanced slowly and my hackles rose.

I shifted my weight to my back paws, ready to flee or fight back if needed. A third wolf growled, louder than the first two, as it approached at a run. It stopped in between its pack mates and looked back and forth, snarling and yapping at them. The first two wolves backed away and lowered their heads, deferring to the newcomer. Something passed between them, some signal I didn't understand, and then all at once, they shifted.

The tawny one became Carter. The dark-brown

one was Brent—my babysitter. The third wolf, the pretty brown one with the shiny coat and pink nose, was Regan—my sister. Figured. I'd all but felt the authority rolling off her the moment she'd appeared.

We both shifted at the same time, her form shimmering at the edges until, with a soft pop of air, we were both human again.

Regan shook her hair out. "What are you doing out here?" she asked me.

"Getting some air," I said.

Brent, even though he was back in human form, was sniffing the air and looking around. "I smell vamp," he said.

"Are you alone out here?" Regan asked. She was standing several feet away, with both guys flanking her, looking every inch an alpha.

I tensed. They did know about vampires. And they hadn't told me. I might be werewolf, like them, but that didn't mean I trusted them. Not like I had immediately trusted the vampire—despite our little fight. And I wasn't going to let them hurt him ... whoever he was.

I met her gaze squarely. "Yes," I said. "I'm alone."

"Huh," Brent grunted, clearly unconvinced.

Regan shot him a look before returning her attention to me. "Look, you can't wander so far from the house. It's not safe."

"Why not?" I asked.

Her eyes bulged. Behind her, Brent and Carter made matching sounds of disappointment. "Don't you know anything about vampires?" Regan demanded.

"No," I said, doing my best to look surprised. "Actually, I don't. In fact, up until now, I didn't even know they existed." It wasn't a lie, not technically.

Regan shook her head. Beside her, Carter muttered something I didn't catch.

"You will," Regan said grimly. Her tone left no doubt in my mind that whatever ill feelings my attacker had for this pack was mutual. "Come on, let's get back. I'll explain on the way."

I hesitated. An hour ago, I would've refused, and taken my chances with running. But now … The vampire was right. I could run away now, but it wouldn't change things. I had to face it head on, like the alpha I might become. And, win or lose, I had to fight for my family. I couldn't just walk away from this chance, especially knowing I might never get it again.

With that in mind, and one last look into the empty woods behind me, I let Regan lead me back.

~8~

REGAN

The meeting hall was crowded even for a meeting like this one. I felt the weight of curious eyes, some concerned, some outright nosy, as I walked into the log building that housed our leader's offices. The building was a long rectangle, nothing fancy, but solid—even now after housing four generations of pack leadership the thick wooden logs and double layer glass was solid and sure. A symbol of our strength, Dad said.

As a kid, I'd come with him and Mom a lot. I'd hang out in the meeting space that made up the atrium of the building, playing in the corners and making forts underneath the tables. I still liked the way it smelled of pine and orange cleaner every time. It was a strange nostalgic comfort to my senses—especially now, with Mom gone.

Still, even as my brain reminded me of it, I looked left automatically as I passed through the entrance. Mom's office was that way. Now Dad's office, I mentally corrected. And not much of her remained. I think it was too painful for him, but I'd still been hurt when he'd cleaned out her things so fast and put them in storage in our attic at home.

But something of her remained. I could feel it in the air as the crowd surged in behind me.

Shoulders jostled mine and I looked up to find Charlie wedged in beside me. She'd been different since I'd caught her running alone in the woods two days ago. Not quite enthusiastic about her fate but more … willing. Although she'd been guarded as well. And something told me Charlie wasn't used to having to be strategic with her words. Still, she was doing it now. And still, every morning she ran alone at dawn.

I hadn't mentioned it to Dad. He'd want her followed, but so far, she always came back. And I knew the importance of privacy when you were constantly in the spotlight, so I let her have it.

"Hey," I said, taking in her pinched mouth and tight brow line. "You okay?"

"There are a lot of … people here," she said, as if admitting a hidden fear.

"This is a bigger turnout than usual," I said, debating how much to say. I was hyper aware of the others nearby who were probably listening to our exchange.

"Why?" Charlie asked.

I nudged her to the right toward our seats as others began to fill into the chairs around us.

"It's the first meeting since … our leadership changed over," I said, dodging the use of the word "Mom."

"Do they want to see if your dad can handle it?" she asked, her word gentle.

"No, they know he can. It's …" I sat and pulled her down beside me, sighing instead of finishing my sentence.

"They are here to see you," she said knowingly. Sympathy broke through her nerves. "Regan, I'm—"

"And you," I added hastily. I hated ruining the moment, but sympathy in front of prying eyes wasn't something I could handle right now. "You're shiny and new and they want to know about you," I added.

"Of course," she said and even though she didn't sound upset to have the subject so abruptly changed, guilt pricked at me for ruining what might've been a nice moment between us.

To assuage my guilt and to fill the silence, I pointed out various elders and pack members as they took their seats. The noise level in the room grew from a hum to a dull roar and I finally left off rather than yell to be heard over it all.

Bevin and Carter entered and I smiled at them. They smiled back and Bevin's gaze swept sideways to Charlie before her smile abruptly died off. I ducked my head, hoping Charlie missed it. No one else spoke to her—or me for that matter—and I wondered if the others felt like Bevin did or if they were keeping their distance out of respect. I wasn't sure, but after that, I purposely kept my gaze averted while we waited for the meeting to begin. For some reason, I felt bad for the less-than-warm reception she was receiving.

Five minutes later, Sheridan's voice cut through the noise in the meeting hall like a whip cracking. "This meeting of the pack will come to order." At the sound of it, half the voices abruptly cut off.

She stood at the head of the table, her usual place despite the fact she wasn't an alpha. I wasn't exactly sure how she'd secured the spot except that Mom seemed to feel it was easier to let Sheridan sit there than to argue over it. Mom always said you had to pick your battles with Sheridan. That she wasn't a woman to take on lightly. I thought Sheridan was a spoiled bitch. All she did was run the meetings. A spokeswoman. A secretary. And not a nice one at that.

The last kid to cross her in one of these meetings had ended up with a patrol line that skirted the sewer plant fifty miles north of here. The route wasn't even in our territory, yet Sheridan had insisted there'd been reports of trespassers coming in that way. The kid had come home smelling like shit for weeks.

When I was alpha, I planned to have her seat moved to the back of the room. Or maybe outside. I hadn't decided which.

I sat in the row behind Dad, at the opposite end of the table from Sheridan. Charlie was on my left in Carter's usual seat. He'd looked pretty pissed to be giving it up, but Dad hadn't given him a choice. These seats were for the higher ranking pack members, which no longer applied to Carter. He wasn't happy about it, either, and let me know it by the silent glare he was aiming at the side of my head from his standing position along the wall. I didn't give him the satisfaction of turning and acknowledging it, and I could tell that pissed him off even more. It's not like it was my decision anyway.

Charlie shifted in her chair. I stole a glance at her out of the corner of my eye. Her dark hair was in a long ponytail down her back, shiny and smooth. I felt a pang of jealousy at the sight of it. I would've loved long hair, but Mom would never allow it. She said it made your wolf too shaggy, which slowed you down. An alpha had to be the fastest in the pack—always.

At least she wasn't wearing a dress anymore. She'd changed into jeans and a sheer blouse over a white tank. It was too feminine for my taste, too much work, but it looked nice on her. Soft, but nice.

"I said, come to order," Sheridan repeated, this time with a distinct edge in her already hard voice.

One by one, the room fell silent under her unforgiving stare.

Across the room my friend, Ronnie, leaned over and whispered something to Lane. She let out a laugh and then clapped her hand over her mouth to hold in the sound. It was too late. Sheridan aimed a cold glare at them and they fell silent with reddening cheeks. I shook my head. Ronnie was forever a flirt even though he'd never managed to convince any of the girls our age to actually date him. And Lane. Her scar—a gift from the Rossi's henchmen—gave her confidence issues that made her an easy target.

Judging from Sheridan's upturned nose, they'd both just made it onto her shit list—maybe literally. I shuddered.

"We are all here to discuss the arrival of Charlotte Vuk, William's daughter," Sheridan began.

"Charlie." She mumbled the correction almost to herself, but made no move to alert Sheridan or the rest of the room. Probably a smart move right about now.

"We welcome you to the pack, Charlotte," Sheridan said to Charlie, a plastic smile frozen to her lips.

"Yes, welcome," Al said. He smiled with what seemed genuine friendliness, but his glittering teeth were a little scary no matter what. Charlie shrank back a little beside me.

"It's lovely to meet you," Sylvia Lantagne said with a nod.

"Thank you," Charlie murmured. I elbowed her and she straightened and cleared her throat. "Thank you," she said again, louder now. "I'm glad to be here."

Sheridan nodded as if satisfied and turned back to the rest of the group before continuing. "As a result of the tragic death of Myra Vuk a few weeks ago, a new alpha must be chosen. William Vuk has been gracious in filling in during this difficult time, but it's a temporary fix. As you all know, the role passes to the ruling female of the household. Up until now, we thought that was Regan." She aimed a nasty slip of a smile at me and I blinked, carefully expressionless.

"But we've since learned that Charlotte is only a few months younger than Regan. Close enough to be equals in the eyes of the pack law on inheritance and alpha leadership. A decision must be made. The law states that in the case of siblings, especially so close in age, a competition shall be held to determine which sibling shall serve."

"I thought the alpha role passed to the eldest living daughter, no exceptions," Carter's dad said. I studied him, trying to read his motivation for asking a question he already knew the answer to, but his calm expression gave away nothing.

"John, you know as well as I do there are provisions in place for twins and the like. While these girls certainly aren't that, their birth dates are close enough to qualify." Carter's dad opened his mouth to argue, but Sheridan cut him off. "Thill and I have already done the research into the archives to determine how this must be handled. We are following the letter of the law." Sheridan shifted again to include the entire room in her response as she said, "We are nothing without our traditions, are we not?"

No one argued.

"Now then, we will welcome Charlotte as a member of the pack. Afford her the same courtesy and respect we do one another. Make her feel at home. She is, after all, one of us," Sheridan finished.

A few pack members glanced at me, but mostly everyone stared at Charlie. A murmur of voices went up. Sheridan managed to quiet them all with a look. Beside me, Charlie kept her eyes on the floor.

"Also being discussed is the agreement made between William, our acting alpha, and Blaine Rossi, regarding the arranged marriage of Blaine's son, Owen, to the new Vuk alpha, whomever that may be."

The room erupted in the sound of exclamations and questions. Sheridan didn't bother trying to quiet them now. She was looking across the table at Dad with a smug expression, and I realized this was the first the pack was hearing about Dad's arrangement.

Temper flared and I leaned forward and hissed at him, "You told us this was a decision agreed upon by the entire Council of Elders."

He twisted in his seat. "Not now, Regan," he said, his voice tight.

"You lied—" I began, too angry to stop now.

He twisted more fully so that our eyes met. His were stormy, holding all of the tension and irritation that his words and body language hid so well. "We will discuss it later. You know all you need to for now."

I sank back against my chair, heat flaring against my cheeks and throat as I realized he'd been holding out on me. Around us, other pack members cried out in protest. I folded my arms, reassured by that. It made me feel a little better that everyone else thought it was just as crazy. Not that any of them could talk him out of it. I knew that look he wore. But I also knew the one Sheridan had aimed at him just now. If anyone could make him change his mind, she had the best chance. She might've been wound too tight, but Dad listened to her.

The room quieted as everyone's initial outbursts faded. Now, the elders took turns voicing their opinion of the deal.

"That's insanity," Al said, bumping his large fist against the oak table in front of him.

Al was a hulking guy with dark skin. His ancestors had come from Europe so his werewolf blood was a little different than ours. His temper was bigger and he could shift quicker than anyone I'd ever seen. The kind of guy you wanted beside you—not opposing you—in a fight.

"You can't just do that without consulting the rest of us," Sylvia said. She tossed her golden hair over her shoulder and shot a look at my father. Sylvia taught dance for the local high school and private lessons for various members of the pack. Her slight build and slender frame were deceiving, though. She could dodge blows faster than any wolf I'd ever seen.

"I can and I did," Dad said calmly. His normally reserved demeanor was even more closed off than usual. I wasn't sure anyone else noticed but I did in the way his rigid shoulders and broad chest didn't even contract with his breathing. He sat perfectly still, a statue of uncompromising authority.

"Wait. He's making his own daughter marry one of *them*?" Lane's voice was full of disgust and disbelief. She'd been leaning against the wall, slouching shoulder to shoulder with Ronnie, but now she straightened and planted her feet. Her dark hair fell in front of her face on one side, not quite covering the scar that marred her cheek.

The wolf inside me felt a twinge of blood lust every time I saw it, a burning desire for revenge against the ones who'd done that to her.

A few chairs down from Charlie, Bevin stuck her finger in her mouth and made a choking sound, like she was pretending to throw up. Some of the other teens laughed.

"William," Sylvia began, her voice lowered to sound reasonable—or to deal with someone she obviously assumed had lost his mind.

"Don't, Sylvia. It's already done," Dad said. Something about the way he'd said it made my breath catch.

"But there was no discussion. No vote," Sylvia said, huffing.

Dad didn't bother to answer her.

Across the table, Sheridan was fiercely intent on the scene but, so far, she remained silent. Beside me, Charlie looked terrified. I couldn't blame her. This wasn't exactly the most pleasant pack meeting, and being her first, I wouldn't be surprised if she bolted soon.

Other pack members chimed in after that, but I noticed none of the other elders did again. They all sat with arms folded and glared down the table at Dad. "What do you mean it's already done?" Sheridan asked, her usual high-pitched voice deadly low.

Silence fell. Someone gasped. My skin crawled as I realized something had happened. Something we couldn't take back.

Thill—the oldest living member of the pack—rose from his seat next to Sheridan and pointed a gnarled finger at Dad.

"You sealed it in blood, didn't you?" The old man's voice was raspy and deep so it was hard to hear from where I sat, but his words hung and seemed to echo in the silence that followed. I felt myself scooting closer to the edge of my seat. I held my breath and crossed my fingers.

No, no, no. He didn't. He wouldn't have…

Dad cleared his throat and met Thill's gaze head on without flinching. "Yes."

There was a collective gasp. I let my shoulders sag and for once I didn't care about holding in my emotions. I dropped my face into my hands and squeezed my eyes shut. There would be no convincing him to change his mind. Not even Sheridan could take this back.

How could he?

"What's the big deal with the blood?" Charlie whispered.

Slowly, I raised my head and looked at her. Her expression was curious and confused. She didn't yet understand there was no hope. The deal was done.

"A blood seal. It's unbreakable. If Dad goes back on it now, they have the right to attack and execute every single one of us. Whether we surrender or not. It's like a death sentence for breaking the law. The council will never go back on a blood deal." I knew my voice sounded bleak. I didn't care. Charlie needed to fully understand. When I was finished, Charlie's expression matched mine.

"Oh," she said.

I felt my chest grow heavy. This was really happening. I was going to get married. To a vampire.

"I can't believe I might have to marry a complete stranger," Charlie said.

Her words startled me.

Did she really think there was a chance it would be her? Did she honestly think she had a shot at beating me in the competition? She knew nothing about being an alpha. Or vampires.

Looking over at her, seeing her misery, I made a decision. I was going to win this competition and save Charlie. I could imagine no fate worse than marriage to a vampire—an immortal, blood-sucking, soulless monster. But for Charlie and for my pack, I would do it. I would be the leader I was raised to be.

And when the competition was over, and I was alpha, I would find a way to save them and destroy the vampires once and for all.

~9~

CHARLIE

I stood stiffly in the center of my room, feeling my trepidation rise as the sun set. I'd spent most of the day to myself. Running—again. For the first hour, I'd pretended I wasn't hoping to see him, but by the end of the second hour when he still hadn't shown, I couldn't hide my disappointment. Out of an entire town full of werewolves, the only person I wanted to spend time with was a vampire; a creature that some innate part of my wolf wanted nothing more than to take a bite out of. Obviously, that feeling had been mutual, probably why he'd continued to stay away.

Still, a friendly face this afternoon would've been nice. Tonight's party loomed like a dark cloud.

Inescapable and heavy with expectations. They hadn't asked me to speak at last night's council meeting but Sheridan looked ready to put me on the spot before that argument had broken out over the marriage.

Even as I thought the word, I shuddered again.

The council meeting had been hell. The air in that roomful of werewolves had become stuffy almost immediately—they'd all stayed in human form, thank goodness—but when their tempers flared, their animals pressed out against the edges and I had felt their strain. After that, I'd purposely kept my eyes away from the door and walls so that I couldn't imagine them closing in on me.

I remembered one especially big guy with dark skin, an elder who made me nervous. His arms had rippled with muscles even when he was sitting still. On top of that, his biceps were larger than both my legs put together.

But then the old man had asked Dad something about sealing the marriage agreement in blood. The silence while they waited for him to answer had been deafening. I'd heard Dad say yes and then the room seemed to tilt. Regan dropped her head into her hands. I watched people's expressions go from angry to resigned to fearful within a single blink.

A sharp knock sounded and before I could pull myself out of my thoughts, Regan pushed through the door. "You okay?" she asked, catching sight of my expression.

"I'm fine," I lied, still distracted.

Regan stepped inside and frowned. Her jeans and boots were all scuffed and muddy. I wanted to ask what she'd been doing but it felt nosy somehow. Even though we lived together, it was all formality. I wasn't actually invited into her life. Better to always remember that than be hurt over and over again.

Regan's boots shuffled against the hardwood and her hands moved as if they were unsure of where to go. She hooked her thumbs in her pockets and stood straight. "Are you nervous about tonight?" she asked quietly.

"Actually, I was wondering about your pack rules and traditions. Are they written down somewhere?" I asked.

"You mean like our law book?" she asked, brows crinkling.

I nodded. "I'd like a copy to read if you have an extra."

"Sure. There's one in the library downstairs. Dad keeps it out for easy reference. The large end table in the back," she said, a distinct note of suspicion lacing her words. Or was it simply curiosity. I couldn't tell with her. "Anything in particular you want to know?"

"There are a lot of things happening here that I don't understand," I said, waving a hand to keep it vague. "It's all so fast paced. I'd like to catch up."

I didn't want to admit that, along with everything else, I was still trying to accept that I actually had the chance to be married at all. I'd convinced myself long ago that marriage and relationships weren't an option for me. And I hated to admit that part of me was glad to know I'd been wrong. Still, if there was a way out of this blind-betrothal mess, a pack law book might hold the answers.

"Uh-huh," Regan said, clearly unconvinced. Fine, she wanted to know my questions, I'd ask them. Regan was probably safer than one of the others.

"For example, what's the big deal with the blood agreement thing Dad made?" I asked.

Regan's eyes flickered with something, but it wasn't surprise. Loathing. Resignation maybe? She hesitated and, for a moment, I wondered if she was even going to answer me. Finally, she sighed and dropped her hands. "It's called a blood seal. Sort of like an oath. It's a way to make an agreement official and binding," she said, and her mouth twisted on the last word. "Anyway, once it's done, it's unbreakable. You can't go back on it if you wanted to."

"Not for any reason?" I asked, hope plummeting a little at that.

"Not unless you feel like dying today," she said with a shrug.

"Wow," I murmured. Regan muttered an agreement that sounded slightly more colorful than mine.

I bit my lip, trying not to drown underneath the reality of my situation. I was going to be forced to compete with my new sister for the title of alpha and then marry another werewolf I'd never met before. All to seal a peace treaty that would guarantee a cease fire for a pack I'd never even met until recently. It wasn't even my war.

"But … isn't that happening anyway?" I asked

almost to myself.

Across from me, Regan looked up and blinked. "What do you mean?"

"Well, isn't this whole marriage idea a way to bring peace between your families?" I asked. "To end some ongoing feud you have with them?" I tried to keep my voice light. I knew this was a sensitive topic for Regan but I honestly just wanted to understand what I'd walked into the middle of.

"It's more than a feud, Charlie," Regan said. She spoke slowly, as if talking to a small child, and I bristled.

"Then maybe you should spell out exactly what it is," I shot back, crossing my arms over my chest. "You walk around spouting a bunch of crap about how the Rossi family is a bunch of monsters, but no one has offered proof of this. I still don't know—"

"Proof?" She straightened, her shoulders stiff and hands balled at her sides. "Proof? No one owes you a damn lick of anything, the least of which is proof. The Rossi family and all of their kind are nothing but … unnatural monsters." She snorted. "I don't have to prove that. Your body will do the work for me."

"What is that supposed to mean?" I asked, more confused than angry at her cryptic explanation. Why would she call her own kind "unnatural?"

"It means get within six feet of one and your wolf will flare up, ready to kill, faster than you can say Regan was right." Her lip curled into something menacing and I wondered if she meant it for me or them. "Our wolves come with a built-in vamp sensor. You'll understand tonight. It'll be all you can do to keep your wolf tucked away inside your gown. In fact, do that, and then find me tomorrow and we'll—"

"Vamp?" I repeated. "Did you just say vamp?" I grabbed at the windowsill to steady myself and tried to clear the dizzy spinning in my head.

"Of course I said vamp. What else did you—oh." She stopped, her eyes widening, and stared at me with her lips parted. "Do you mean none of us … We failed to mention that tiny detail, didn't we?"

I nodded, a hand pressed to my stomach to calm the swirling nausea. The Rossi family … the monsters who killed her mother … the unnatural creatures that sparked an automatic kill order in our werewolf side … and my new friend in the woods—all the same.

One of us was going to marry a murdering vampire.

"The Rossi family is the royal family of the vampires—and our future in-laws," she explained.

"I see." I straightened and found Regan watching me closely, as if waiting for something.

Her head tilted sideways in curiosity. "Did you think the engagement was between another wolf?"

I nodded again, this time reddening from my embarrassment. "Sorry," Regan muttered and blew out a breath.

I focused on breathing too but only until I couldn't hear my pulse roaring in my ears.

I straightened and met Regan's concerned gaze. "You good?" she asked.

I waited a beat to be sure and then nodded.

“Really glad you cleared all that up for me before tonight’s soiree,” I said when I found my voice.

Regan snorted and slowly, our mouths broke out into matching grins. “Right. That would’ve been an awkward reaction as you shook hands with the future in-laws.”

I giggled and there was something half-mad about the sound. I wondered if I’d just reached some sort of breaking point in what I could handle. And if so, would that make things easier or harder from now on.

“Tonight’s going to be hard,” Regan said, her smile finally diminishing into something that looked an awful lot like concern.

My own humor died instantly. I looked away—back toward the view from my window where caterers were setting up for what my dad had officially labeled the engagement party. I stared down at the string lights and tin lanterns being hung from tree branches until the weight of Regan’s stare prompted me to break the silence.

“Will we have to say anything?” I asked. “Tonight, I mean. In front of everyone.”

“I don’t think so,” she said. “Dad will probably make a speech. Maybe Mr. Rossi. You’ll have to make small talk with them. And you’ll have to keep from killing them all even though you’ll want to,” she added in a wry voice.

I sighed and finally tore my gaze away from my window. “Thanks, Regan,” I said.

“For what?” she asked, blinking in surprise.

“For always telling me the truth,” I said. “If we weren’t … If things were different, you’d be a cool sister," I admitted, ignoring the pang I felt as I said the words aloud.

To my surprise, Regan's eyes clouded. "Thanks. You too," she whispered.

The silence felt awkward and I waited until Regan got ahold of herself, pretending not to notice when she used the corner of her sleeve to wipe her lids dry.

I cleared my throat. "So about that book," I said.

"I'll have someone bring it right up," she said quickly, already edging toward the door. "See you tonight," she added.

"See you tonight," I echoed as she slipped out.

-10-

REGAN

Brent's expression as he came in the front door was sour—even for him. "Can you take this up to Charlie?" I asked, thrusting the thick volume into his hands as I walked out of the library.

"What is it?" He peered down at the weathered spine even though we both already knew. There was only one book that looked like that. The pack law book was thick and old. Maybe even older than Thill. Brent handled it carefully as he turned it over. "Why does Charlie want this?" he added.

"To play catch up," I said, even though I already knew it was more than that. I'd seen it in her eyes when she'd asked me. She wanted to find a loophole to this whole contest thing. I couldn't blame her. "Can you take it up to her?"

"I'm on my way," he grunted, already heading for the stairs. One thing about Brent, he didn't waste words.

I moved past him toward the front door. My job here was done, at least until tonight's soiree. For now, I needed air. To be alone. And woods. My wolf needed to breathe.

My hand on the knob, I paused at the sound of Brent's voice calling down to me. "You headed anywhere in particular?" he asked.

I shrugged. "Just out."

"Do yourself a favor and avoid the back acre." He grimaced. "It already smells like vermin."

"Will do." I saluted him in thanks. "Later," I said and slipped out into the front yard.

The porch creaked in all its usual places as I bounded down the steps onto the grass. I turned away from the hillside with the view of town and took a right toward the forest.

Three steps in, I realized Brent was right. The air was ripe with visiting humans and the promise of vampires. A catering truck was parked behind our pickup, blocking me in. Just as well. I'd rather run. But with all these people around setting up for tonight, I needed to be discreet.

I slipped quietly between two dollies loaded down with champagne and coolers for the outdoor bar Dad had ordered. No one looked twice and even as the alpha in me bristled at being ignored, I was grateful for the anonymity that came with being a teenager in a world full of adults.

The air inside the forest was cooler and damp

in the fading afternoon. Lengthy shadows ran like columns between thick redwoods. I inhaled the sweet scent of pine and wet bark and exhaled what I hoped was all the bullshit clogging up my normally clear head.

Dad hadn't spoken to me since the council meeting. Not because he was ashamed or guilty for the blood oath. He was pissed at me for physically reacting—challenging him, he'd said to me on the way home last night. It was the last thing he'd said. I was too twisted up to care.

Part of me hoped Charlie did find something in that book to stop this madness.

Leaves crunched behind me, soft but loud enough for my heightened wolf senses to balk at. I whirled, halfway to shifting as I scanned for the threat.

"Relax, boss. It's just me," Carter said as he stepped around one of the larger tree trunks at the edge of the path.

My shoulders sagged and I exhaled, stuffing my wolf back inside. "I almost killed you," I said as he came up beside me.

His mouth quirked. "You almost tried," he corrected.

When I didn't react to his humor, his smile faded and he bent closer, searching my face. "What is it?" he asked. "Did something happen?"

I shook my head at that. Something else. Because my mother's murder, a duel against my sister, and impending nuptials to an abomination didn't qualify. There had to be something else. But he was right. We were both sort of waiting for the other shoe to drop. Instead of answering, I turned away and kicked the tree, wincing at the throb it left behind. But I welcomed the pain—needed it considering the swirling mess of my insides.

"Regan, talk to me," Carter said, stepping closer and reaching for my elbow. He spun me around to face him and I blinked up into his blue eyes, intent with worry. The familiarity of his gaze, of the scent of him—years of friendship and trust—made my throat close. Charlie hadn't had any of this. Coming into the pack had been her first real shot at it. And here I was, basically taking it all away from her again.

She had no idea what she'd been thrust into—or what she was up against. And I couldn't do much to help her either. Not while I fell into the category of her opponent.

"It's Charlie," I said and Carter's grip relaxed by a few inches. Clearly, he'd been expecting something worse—whatever that was.

I slipped free and turned away again, kicking at the dirt as I wandered along. Carter followed behind me, but I didn't meet his gaze. Some part of me was too embarrassed. He was right. There were much worse problems than Charlie's adjustment.

"What about her?" he asked.

"She … she's foreign," I said finally. "Not an inch of experience or knowledge of our world. Her world," I corrected with a frown. "She's lived her entire life with humans, completely clueless that anyone else like her even existed."

"And that bothers you?" Carter asked, his tone way too gentle and understanding for my liking. It only made my concern more real.

I huffed. “It’s going to get her killed. Or worse.”

“Worse?” Carter echoed.

I whirled, choosing temper over concern. “Apparently in all our instruction about the Rossi monsters, we failed to actually explain they were vampires. She was oblivious. Almost walked right into the party tonight unaware. She could’ve killed one of them if she hadn’t been on guard, prepared to restrain herself.”

“Shit.” Carter let out a low whistle. “We dropped the ball on that one.”

“How can Dad expect her to survive here, much less compete? She’s never even hunted before. She can’t win and it’s going to humiliate her and alienate her from the pack even more.”

“I’m sorry, Regan,” Carter said. “What can I do?”

I look up at him, surprised. “You would help her?”

“Of course.”

“Why?” I asked, too shocked to put it more delicately.

“Because it would be helping you. You’re my alpha. The boss,” he said, attempting a joke. I half-smiled, but it disappeared too fast.

“Tonight. At the party, will you keep an eye on her?” I asked. “Make sure she doesn’t get into trouble with one of them. Or Dad’s agenda for her, whatever that is.”

“You want me to hang out with Charlie all night?” His brows crinkled and he pressed his lips together.

"Is that too much?" I asked.

"No, I just thought … I was going to offer to do the same for you. Escort you," he added. A slight flush tinged his cheeks and I stared at it in confusion. Carter was embarrassed? For what?

"I think Charlie needs a babysitter more than I do," I said.

"I wasn't— I meant that you and I would … Yeah, okay," he said, running a hand through his light hair until it stood up on end. He looked away, suddenly not meeting my gaze. Something felt off, though I had no idea what.

"Okay," I echoed.

In the silence, Carter's mouth thinned. "What is it, Carter?" I prompted when he only continued to glare into the trees.

"I hate that your dad did this behind your back. Or at all. Marriage? To a vamp? It's …"

"Horrific, I know," I said, watching the way his nostrils flared and his fists bunched. His form shivered at the edges, his wolf pressing up and out, and I knew he was seriously pissed. "Calm down," I said. "We'll figure it out."

"I hope so." He grunted, muttering something under his breath that I missed.

"What did you say?" I asked.

"Nothing. Look … I've been thinking. We can fight this if you want. You have the support of the younger generation. Me, Bevin, Lane, all the others stand behind you. We'll do what you say in order to change their minds."

Alarm speared through me as I realized what he

meant. “What? Like a rebellion or mutiny or something?”

“I wouldn’t call it that, but we would break away. Leave if we had to—”

“No.” I shook my head. “Absolutely not. We are not starting an uprising. Not now.” I looked around, half-terrified my father was standing close enough to hear this nonsense.

Carter wasn’t deterred. “Even Bevin agrees, if we work together—”

“Bevin still thinks Justin Bieber was the most influential figure of 2012,” I hissed. “We are not taking political or tactical advice from her.”

Carter sighed. “Fine. I just want you to know you have our loyalty.”

“As friends,” I corrected meaningfully. “But your ultimate loyalty is to the pack. Not one person, certainly not me. And I am not doing this. We are part of a whole. Without the whole, the part is only pieces.” Carter blinked and finally relaxed.

“Who said that?” he asked.

“My mother,” I said quietly. “And she was right. Please don’t bring that up again.”

“I won’t,” he said. “And your mom was right. But … Regan, for me, you are the whole.”

My heart thudded irregularly. “What does that mean?” I asked.

Again, Carter’s cheeks flushed pink. “Just that … whatever. I’ll see you tonight.”

“Okay. I’ll see you tonight,” I said slowly, still lost. Or maybe it was terror that sent my pulse racing as he shifted uncomfortably. I looked at the buttons on his shirt, unwilling to meet his eyes as the girl side of my brain attempted to decode his words. Did Carter mean more than just declarations of leadership? I'd thought he was speaking as a true beta, a supporter, a second in command. But something about the way he'd said it made me think maybe he meant more than that.

"See you," Carter mumbled, turning on his heel and melting into the greenery until I was once again alone.

-11-

CHARLIE

Daylight faded slowly until long shadows forced me to use the bedside lamp in order to make out the soft scrawls that filled the pages of the pack's law book. Page after dusty page held handwritten notes scribed in varying versions of English from Olde to modern to legal contract language. The rules and customs of these people were endless and, at times, contradicting. But the running theme throughout was that the alpha was the final word. Every time. If I hadn't seen a council meeting first hand and watched the alpha allow others to speak their minds—including disagreements—I would have been convinced this was a very oppressive dictatorship.

The more I read, the tighter my nerves twisted. Not only was there absolutely no sign of a loophole for this contest business, my future was about to become very different than my past. Regan had been right. It was normal for us to be taken from public school from high school on. Pack responsibilities came first. There were entire chapters dedicated to hunting and others to patrolling and what to do if a trespasser stumbled upon our side of the territory line. How to handle challenges to your pack position. Politics. Elections for elder officers. You name it, the book had it. All except the marriage thing. That had never been done.

But vampires. Monsters. Freaks of nature—the book described them as all of these—were not scarce. I lingered over that section, wanting to learn all I can, but it only listed the basics about their makeup: They drank blood to survive. Sunlight didn't harm them but it did tire them more quickly. They were our natural enemy. Our wolves literally tasted the need for violence when we smelled their kind. It was built in to destroy them. Underneath that, the book laid out different ways to kill them.

I scanned those lines with a subtle sickness roiling my gut. I wanted to know but I also didn't. That vampire in the woods had been my friend. Tonight, they wouldn't be. But Regan had warned me against lashing out. Tonight we were here to make peace.

My eyes caught on the last line of every technique. Apparently, burning them was the only way to assure their destruction. Great, so

Hollywood had at least gotten that part right.

At the sound of a sharp knock, I flinched and snapped the thick volume shut.

"Yes?" I called.

Brent poked his head inside, his eyes flickering from me to the book that lay on the mattress in front of me. Finally, I caught him check my bedside clock. "You should start preparing for tonight," he said. "They'll be expecting you soon."

"Right," I said, startled to realize how late it had gotten while I read. "I'll be ready," I added, shoving the book aside as Brent slipped out again.

I got up and went to the window, nerves tightening further as I spotted all of the foot traffic coming and going on the foot path that ran parallel to my side of the house. Carts and coolers and men in black pants and crisp button-ups trickled steadily back and forth toward what I'd heard them refer to as the back acre.

Dad was going all out for this thing. My engagement party. I wrinkled my nose and turned back, sighing as I went to the closet to retrieve my dress. A plum number Regan had brought up this morning. It wasn't a color I would've chosen for myself. It suited her more. I suspected it might've once been hers.

My first hand-me-down, I realized with a frown.

I dressed quickly.

The moment it was dark, they would expect me to come downstairs, walk through the neighborhood under the scrutiny of dozens of expectant eyes, and meet the mortal enemies of a pack I didn't want to have anything to do with. To prevent war, bloodshed, and the death of a hundred innocent lives, I reminded myself. Somewhere along the way in my reading, I'd realized how close to that we really were. Regan was convinced these monsters had killed her mom. The history in that book had taught me what a betrayal that was. Not just taking a life—the life of an alpha was precious enough to warrant swift and harsh retaliation. In fact, I was surprised they hadn't done anything about it yet.

Maybe Dad was right; this marriage was the only thing holding the violence at bay.

"No pressure," I whispered to my empty room.

That wasn't even the thing that had me the most stressed, although I guess the whole war thing should have been the worst of my worries. The idea of death and destruction sucked. But more than all of that, I was breathless with the idea of possibly seeing my stranger in the woods again. Did he know anything about Regan's mom's murder?

I stood at the mirror toying with my hair and trying not to think about any of it. But the more I attempted anything fancy, the more nervous I became. I needed Mom. She'd always been my hairstylist. Finally, my hair fully rebelled and I gave up. I'd wear it down.

And maybe tomorrow, I'd finally call her. Let her explain herself. And find a way to tell her that despite being kidnapped and forced into this, I'd gone completely crazy and decided to stay. That last part had held me back from dialing her for days now.

I took a final look at my reflection, squaring

my shoulders in an attempt at a power pose. I thought of Regan and how she didn't need to do anything different to power pose. It was already built in somehow. At that, my shoulders slumped.

Someone moved behind my reflection and I whirled, eyes wide. Regan stood in my doorway, hand still hovering on the knob.

"Sorry," she said. "Didn't mean to scare you."

"It's fine, I was just … finishing up with my dress. It's lovely," I said.

She nodded but otherwise ignored the gift. "The alpha is an important figure in a lot of ceremonies. We had to make sure you looked the part."

The part. I thought again of the power pose and noted how she stood naturally with shoulders back, chin up. Embarrassment washed over me. I felt as though she'd caught me dressing up in Mom's clothes.

"You look great," I said in an attempt to shift the spotlight.

And she did. My sister looked amazing—every inch the alpha. Her dress was practical. It had a scoop neck, lacing up the front, and a loose skirt that was made for movement. Sparkly gemstones were pinned to her short hair that matched the detail on her breast. The brown material should have made her look plain, but instead, it made her look mature and powerful.

Insecurity gnawed at me. I would never look that self-assured. Maybe they were all right to assume she would win the alpha contest.

"Thanks," she said, a half-smile pulling one

side of her lips up in what looked like a mixture of surprise and pleasure. “The rest of your things were brought up at lunch. Did you find them?”

“My things?” I asked in confusion. Did she mean the homecoming dress they’d brought me here in? That thing had to have been trashed after everything—

“Dad ordered some new things for you until you could shop for yourself,” Regan explained. “They’re in the wardrobe. I assumed you would’ve found them by now or I would’ve told you earlier. Your mom helped pick them out.”

“My mom?” I said, crossing to the wardrobe and yanking it open. Some part of me half-expected her to be in there along with the clothes. It was silly, but my heart sank anyway at seeing only fabric hanging. Still, even at first glance I saw that it was high-quality fabrics.

“Thank you. Wow,” I said, fingering through the blouses and dresses hanging inside. “These are great.”

“Dad said your mom ordered from your favorite store.”

“He spoke to her?” I asked, turning sharply.

“Sure. We wanted to let her know you were all right,” Regan said. “You still haven’t called her, have you?” she asked, her voice gentling.

“No,” I said, staring down at my fingers twisting in front of me. Guilt pricked at me over it, but not as heavy as before. At least she knew I was all right.

“I’m sure she’ll be glad to hear from you, when you’re ready,” Regan offered.

I didn't answer. I couldn't tell her I wasn't ready. Not when I knew she'd never be able to talk to her own mother ever again. It didn't seem right to complain about mine. I looked through the wardrobe again and my eyes caught on a lacy dress far in the back.

I yanked the other hangers aside and traced my fingers down the bodice of a finely beaded white dress. It took me a few seconds and a full sweep of the garment to realize what it was. "Wait. Is this…?" I snapped my hand away as Regan came up beside me.

"That's for the wedding," she said quietly, confirming my worst fears. I looked up and found my terror mirrored back at me in her expression. "There wouldn't be time to have one made between the end of the competition and the ceremony, so we both have one. Just in case."

My stomach flip-flopped with nerves. I already had my wedding dress. This was too weird.

"I don't know if…" I stopped, struggling to form the words without also giving way to tears. "I decided to stay and do this but … every time I think I can, something else happens and—" I broke off, but Regan nodded.

"If it makes you feel any better, I feel the same way," she said.

I attempted a smile. "It does. Thank you."

She searched my face, but instead of intrusive, her onceover felt friendly. Almost caring. "Is there anything else you need before tonight…?"

I sniffled—the only evidence of my freak out, which was progress for me. "I couldn't find any mascara anyway."

"Sure. I left you some things in the vanity. Waterproof?" she asked.

"Please," I said with a wry smile.

"Let me help you." Regan moved through my room, collecting makeup from the bathroom I hadn't known was there and helping me with the top button of the dress. Afterward, she did my hair with deft fingers, piling some of it on top of my head and leaving the rest loose.

I stared at the wall over her shoulder while she swept liner along my eyelid. She smelled like powder and soil, beautiful but earthy.

"Don't worry," she said in a gentle voice as she worked. "Tonight's going to be easy."

"Easy?" I gave a shaky laugh. "I think we have different definitions of the word."

Regan smiled tightly. "Open your mouth and look up."

I obeyed, and she finished the rest of my eye makeup just as swiftly and confidently as she had done my hair. Once the lip gloss was brushed on, she stepped back to let me see myself in the mirror again.

The reflection looked nothing like me.

I scrutinized myself in the mirror, turning my chin this way and that so I could see my hair and face from all angles. I looked like a stranger, someone not-quite-Charlie, like maybe Regan had cloned herself with longer hair. When I straightened my back and held my shoulders straight, I passed for confident. Almost like an alpha, too.

I just hoped it would be enough for whatever

was expected of me. Now that it was time, the nerves returned, full force now. I clamped down and lectured myself about not throwing up.

"You look good," Regan said, breaking my reverie.

"Yeah. I guess," I said, terror leaching away at my confidence already.

Disappointment flashed across her face, then vanished fast enough that I thought I might have imagined it. "We should get going," she said.

"Hey, Regan," I called and she paused in the doorway. "I was wondering … I mean, I read over the book you sent up and couldn't find anything about this…"

"What is it?" she asked.

"Our contest for alpha. They say it's required to determine the new leader, but what if I refuse? I mean, forfeit. Wouldn't they just give it to you and then I'm beta and no one has to fight about it?"

Regan's expression didn't lift like I'd hoped. There was no relief as she regarded me, nothing like I'd hoped. "That's not—It doesn't work like that, Charlie," she said and I could hear the regret in her voice.

"How does it work then?" I asked.

"If you forfeit you would lose your place here. They would remove you. Send you home."

"Well, I mean, what's so bad about that?" I asked, and even without asking I knew there was a catch coming. It was in her tone.

"You would never be allowed to return or have communication with any of us. Including your family. And … I would…" She sighed.

"You would what?" I prompted. "What happens to you?"

"The Vuk line would no longer have a rightful claim to the alpha role. It would pass to the next in line," she said, pain twisting her words and her expression. It was easy to see how much it cost her even to consider the possibility and my heart panged.

"What if I threw the fight?" I asked.

Regan hesitated. "You would do that?" she asked quietly.

"I don't want to fight you," I said.

Regan bit her lip and finally, she shook her head. "I don't think that's wise. If they find out we planned it, we'd both be disqualified anyway. Besides, it's not all a physical battle. There will be mental challenges, and without knowing ahead of time what's coming, it's too risky to try and throw it."

"I see," I said. "Well, I was just wondering."

Regan nodded. "Let's get going before we're late."

I followed quickly, eager to put the conversation behind us.

Together, we left the main house and walked along into the woods behind the house. Big paper lanterns had been draped in the trees with flickering tea lights inside of them. They illuminated a sparkling path to the clearing where all the benches had been set up.

A band played on the stage. Waiters—other werewolves dressed in nice coats and slacks—were walking around with drinks on trays. I snagged one as they passed and drank the whole thing at once. Sparkling apple cider. It wouldn't do anything for my nerves but I needed something to do.

Regan watched me through it all with critical eyes.

"Okay," I said, squaring my shoulders. "Let's meet the in-laws."

-12-

REGAN

Charlie looked amazing. Seeing the way she sparkled in a dress like that made me wonder how different things would've been had we grown up as a pair.

I hated dresses. Almost as much as I hated parties. Everyone wandering around to the beat of watered-down elevator music and flashing their pasted-on smiles at each other, making small talk about the weather or who had the better patrol schedule ... All so they could try to one-up each other on who had worn the more expensive dress. A complete waste of time and alcohol.

But Charlie took it all in like a kid on Christmas morning. When we broke through the trees into the lantern-lit clearing, I heard her gasp, felt her footsteps stall. Her eyes grew round, and even though she tried to hide it, I could tell the sight in front of us only made her feel more out of place.

Something protective welled up inside me, something I hadn't even known was there, and suddenly all I wanted to do was turn around and take her home. Out of instinct I scanned the crowd, cataloguing the faces into two groups. Us. And them.

Charlie took a few steps forward into the crowd and I followed, still scanning and counting. There was Sheridan huddled in the far corner with my father. Her face was scrunched, like she'd just eaten something sour, which probably meant she was still fussing at him for the deal he'd made. Good. Finally, Sheridan and I saw eye to eye on something.

Across the clearing from them, on the far side of a dance floor that had been constructed, stood Blaine and Gretchen Rossi. Both of them were the epitome of "pale and brooding" with their translucent skin and black formal wear. They were flanked by two men; their security detail, I assumed. I scanned their group for their son, Owen, but he was nowhere in sight. That made a nerve in my neck twitch. As usual with their close proximity, my wolf strained to break free, but I shoved it back and continued my watchful inspection. I needed to see who was here and where they stood. My wolf couldn't handle any surprises.

Goose bumps rose on the back of my neck and I jerked around. Carter stood several feet behind us decked out in a dark suit complete with a forest-green tie. I liked the color contrast. Woods, earthy, animal. Nothing like *them.* His hair had been combed back in a classic gentleman's style that I found myself admiring before I realized I was staring and turned away.

When I glanced back again, he raised his drink, eyes sparkling with something I didn't recognize as his gaze swept the length of me. A shiver ran down my back at the way he studied me. Just like I'd done, he finally caught himself and blinked away whatever had been there a moment ago. Glass still raised, he used it to salute me before nodding toward Charlie.

I understood. He would shadow us until he was needed closer. He would watch her tonight like I'd asked. I nodded back in thanks.

Unaware of the exchange or her bodyguard, Charlie tugged on my elbow and leaned in. "I feel like biting someone," she said with a frown as she looked around at the pale faces.

I snickered. Charlie wasn't even a little bit scary or violent. If *she* felt like tearing something apart limb from limb, that's you knew it was bad. "Join the club," I muttered.

"You mean pack."

The sarcastic bite in her words drew my attention back to Charlie. She reached out and selected a glass of the sparkling cider from one of the waiters passing by and knocked it back in one swig. I watched as her face registered surprise and then disappointment. She was apparently hoping for alcohol. She wouldn't realize that would be a huge mistake in a gathering like this one.

"Okay. Let's meet the in-laws," she said.

I tried to ignore the punch of angry heat that term created in my gut. I led Charlie through the crowd, aiming loosely for where my father stood with Sheridan. We got stopped several times along the way, mostly because of Charlie. Sylvia was a glitter bomb of shimmer and smiles in her champagne-colored slip gown. Al hulked over us in a suit sans jacket. I suspected he couldn't find one that would fit around his massive arms. We were probably lucky he'd found a shirt to button.

They waylaid us with polite questions and avid curiosity. Everyone wanted to meet the long-lost Vuk heir. I secured my smile firmly in place and did my duty with the introductions, trying not to gag on the small talk. Charlie answered everything they threw at her and for that, I was impressed. Maybe even proud. But now wasn't the time to say so. Instead, I stuck close beside her, ready to rescue if needed. By the time we made it to Dad, Sheridan's voice had risen and her expression was fiery as she faced him.

"You're insane, William, if you think a truce will last. Blaine's probably using tonight as a way to scope out our defenses. Pinpoint our weak spots. I can't believe you'd blood seal this thing. And without putting it to the elders—"

"Myra wanted it this way, Sheridan," Dad said, his tone unusually placating. Or was that exhaustion I heard. "It was her idea. And now … with her gone … All that matters is getting the new alpha in place." He was surprisingly calm for the level of heat Sheridan had aimed at him. But I couldn't think past his first statement. My mother had set this up? Really?

"We know who killed Myra. They're standing right over there." Sheridan gestured across the dance floor with a nod of her head.

"Blaine didn't do this," Dad said and the certainty in his words made me pause.

Charlie's eyes widened as we stepped up next to them, but I kept silent. Did he really believe they were innocent? What did he know that we didn't? And why had Mom hidden so much from me?

"Then who did it, William? Is there another vampire coven we're at war with?" Sheridan demanded, too caught up in their discussion to notice us. "Because Myra, *my* best friend, had two holes in her neck when you found her. Last I checked, that was pretty indicative of a vamp." Sheridan's voice rose loud enough on the last word that a few others—werewolf and vampire alike—turned their heads to look.

I shot a look at Charlie and she glanced back at me with a single brow raised. Guilt worked its way along my gut as I realized I'd been caught in my lie. I'd told Charlie Mom was stabbed—it was technically true. Stabbed by fangs. The knife wound story was the official one that we'd given to police and outsiders. And the day I'd told Charlie, as far as I was concerned, she'd still been an outsider.

For now, I offered a subtle shake of my head and an apology in my expression. Charlie turned away, and I knew she'd let it go for now. I'd have to apologize later.

"Lower your voice, Sheridan." Dad smiled—one of his fake, political ones. "We're at a party, remember? An engagement party, to be exact." He turned so easily that I knew he'd been aware of us the entire time. "And here are my girls now."

Dad turned to me and I returned his smile with one of my own. It felt just as forced and plastic as his. God, I hated parties. And politics. "Hi, Dad."

"Regan. You look beautiful, as always." He turned to Charlie and his eyes flickered over her. His smile deepened to something more genuine. "Charlotte, you look ... breathtaking."

A pang of jealousy twisted in my gut. I swallowed, shoving it down.

I couldn't stand there and watch my dad fawn over Charlie. I felt inadequate enough being next to her.

"Excuse me," I said, stepping away. My sister watched me go. Dad didn't even look.

The clearing was uncomfortably full with a large empty space slicing through. It was as though an invisible line had been drawn down the center of the forest. My pack was crowded on one side, forming a solid wall of impenetrable bodies, and then several feet away, the vampires watched with hungry eyes.

I found a vantage point at the back of the crowd where the hill sloped up a little, letting me watch everyone. Whatever the elders said about a truce, I didn't trust a fight not to break out. Too many of us felt like Sheridan—hungry for violence even without our wolves' reflexes begging for it. I needed to be ready to intervene.

The vampires weren't really any taller than the rest of us, but they seemed to take up so much more space in the clearing. Darkness radiated from them. A chill in the air. They were venomous snakes in the grass, and we had invited them onto our land and into our home. And I would have to marry one of them. The very thought of it gave me a sour taste in the back of my mouth.

I glared at Blaine and Gretchen Rossi as they sipped champagne and laughed, like they hadn't a care in the world. It was a ruse. It had to be.

But where was that prince of theirs?

My eyes flicked to Charlie. She looked so small among everyone else, and protectiveness rocked me to the bone. I couldn't let her marry a vampire. I just couldn't. Even if I didn't outweigh her in every category, I would still find a way to beat her. Somehow, she'd gotten underneath my skin and made me care about her.

Several feet back, I found Carter. Still sipping and watching Charlie while also scanning the surrounding area and beyond. His searching led him directly to me and our eyes met—as if he'd already known where I was. His green eyes sparkled brightly even from this distance as his expression lightened. Not quite a smile, but a little less worry lines along his forehead. I waved and he waved back before finally turning away to listen to whatever Bevin was saying to him.

A hush rippled through the crowd on both sides.

A new vampire stepped into the clearing. It was like he'd appeared out of shadow; empty space one minute and then the next, he was just there. His shoulders were almost as wide as he was tall, his hair buzzed close to his scalp in some version of a military cut, and angry red eyes scanned the gathering. Not the prince—I recognized the heavy signet ring on one hand with the royal family's seal, which meant he was in their service. He was a brute. A bodyguard. The Rossi killing machine, I'd heard some of my pack call him.

And a moment later, I saw why he had come.

The leaves rustled unnaturally in the still air. The hush turned to a vibration of expectancy. The vampires, in particular, watched with upturned faces, red eyes sparkling.

The brute moved aside in deference as Prince Owen himself stepped into the clearing.

-13-

CHARLIE

Like a switch had been flipped, everyone fell quiet all at once. I stretched up on my toes to see what was happening, but I was too short. All I could see were the back of people's heads before they gave way to trees.

"What's going on?" I asked.

"The prince is here," Dad muttered. He squeezed my shoulder. "I need to speak to Gretchen and Blaine Rossi. Why don't you wait here for now, Charlotte?"

He disappeared into the crowd before I could manage to say, "It's Charlie."

I wasn't comfortable with my dad yet, but having him close was familiar, if nothing else. With him and Regan gone, I felt like I was adrift in a hostile sea. The elders were staring at me. It was like they expected me to suddenly perform a stupid pet trick—flip over on my back and balance plates on my nose or something. The mental imagery was so dumb that I had to fight not to laugh.

The music restarted and slowly, the chattering began again. Whatever grand entrance this prince had made was done and the party resumed. Still, no one approached me and I shuffled to the fringes, trying to decide what to do next. Voices swirled around me. Sheridan had given up on her argument and sat at a table in hushed conversation with the wrinkled old man beside her. Thill, they'd called him. Snippets of conversations reached me. I ignored most of them but one comment in particular caught my attention.

"I can't believe Regan is going to have to marry that monster. Maybe she can kill him when he falls asleep on their wedding night."

I searched through the small huddles of guests until I found the speaker. She had light-brown hair, shoulder length, and a pointy chin. Her eyes were the same exact shade of green as Carter's. I remember seeing them sitting together behind us at the council meeting. I assumed this must be Bevin, Carter's sister; the one who planned on helping Regan train for the competition.

"Dummy. Vamps don't sleep," said the girl beside her. She was small and slender and had her hair cut shorter than Bevin's, in a pixie cut.

Bevin snorted. "That explains the dark circles under their eyes."

I turned back to the front before they could notice me listening in. I kept my expression carefully neutral and stared down at my hands. The sureness in Bevin's voice sparked anger in me. She was acting like it wasn't even a question that Regan would win and become the alpha.

What about me? I had a chance. It might be small compared to her. I might not have the fighting skills or hunting skills she did (the thought of killing and eating something in my wolf form made me want to gag), but it was possible. Or it could be. If I wanted it.

And for some reason, the knowledge that I'd been so easily counted out had awakened competitiveness inside me I hadn't known was there. After what Regan said earlier, I couldn't bring myself to entertain the idea of forfeiting any longer, but I refused to be cast out of the running so easily. I could at least put up a fight, show them I should be taken seriously.

If I was ever going to belong somewhere, Paradise was it.

I made a decision. I would learn to fight. And hunt. And I would find out everything I could about leading a pack. If it meant I had to marry this Owen guy, I'd do it. No more daydreaming about a friendly vampire in the woods. I would be loyal only to my pack and somehow, I'd earn their loyalty back.

I was a Vuk. It was time I acted like it.

"I'm going to go find a drink," I said to no one in particular and stomped off.

There wasn't a drop of alcohol in the clearing.

It was all apple cider and punch. Punch? In a gathering of werewolves? I couldn't believe it. I would have been much more prepared to find glasses of blood or something for the vampires.

I found a mostly unoccupied buffet table and stationed myself next to it, snacking on grapes and scanning the crowd. Everyone who passed gave me a hard look but I ignored them. What was I supposed to do? Wave to the crowd like the Queen of England?

"Why is such a beautiful creature standing all alone?"

I whirled at the familiar voice. The vampire I had met at the clearing had somehow materialized at my back. I hadn't even seen him arrive to the party. He had been dark and handsome the last time I saw him, but it was nothing compared to the way he looked now. He wore a black suit cut close to the lines of his body that accentuated his slim figure. A brush of hair fell over his eyes—I tried not to dwell on his red irises. Heavy gold rings marked his fingers, the kind of jewelry that was passed down through generations of family. The only splash of color in his suit was a crimson tie. Definitely dressed to impress.

"You! What are you doing here?"

"I could ask the same of you," he said, circling me slowly. I could feel him behind me even when I couldn't see him, like he was trailing a hand along my back. I closed my eyes and shivered, ignoring my wolf as it warned me not to turn my back on my new friend.

"Don't you know this is a dangerous

gathering?" His voice came from my left but still, I pretended to be unconcerned and stared ahead.

"It's supposed to be a party," I said.

"You don't believe that, do you?"

I shook my head. When I opened my eyes, he was standing right in front of me, his chin tilted as he studied me, and it was all I could do to keep breathing. His eyes glimmered. But this time, the red had nothing to do with my fascination. Instead, my attention caught on the way they were focused on my lips.

I couldn't help it. I had to touch the arm of his suit. It was spun from fine silk, and I was willing to bet I had never touched anything so expensive in my life. Slowly, I reached out a tentative hand and let my fingers brush along the silky fabric. The moment I did, my senses seemed to come awake and I jerked my hand back as my cheeks heated in a blushed.

The vampire was looking at the place I touched him, but now a few others were watching. I didn't have to look up to know. I felt it just like I'd felt him. My wolf growled inside me, warning me just *what* it was that watched us.

"This is a mistake," I whispered.

His hand brushed my chin. "The party, or…?"

"All of it," I said quickly.

"You have no clue how much I agree, darling," he murmured. His hungry gaze raked down my body. "You look beautiful."

My cheeks heated, but instead of retreat, I planted my heeled feet and stood my ground. I'm a Vuk, I reminded myself. I couldn't run away from my first vamp encounter, especially in front of so many onlookers. "You look pretty good too," I said, forcing my voice light and uncaring. "So how are you related to the family anyway? You're not with those uptight royals, are you?" I turned my nose up in obvious distaste.

His laughter rang out like the chime of bells. It was surprisingly pleasant and lit up his face. "Uptight royals, hmm? I like that. I'm with them, but believe me when I say it's not by choice."

"Yeah, we can't choose our family," I muttered, shooting a glance at my dad. He was in the middle of a tense conversation with the vampire king and queen, but all of their eyes were trained on me. I shivered as the strange vampire leaned in, either unaware or uncaring of our audience.

"No matter how much we wish we could," he added softly.

Our eyes connected. I recognized that expression of distress and resignation. For the second time since I had been abducted to Paradise, I felt like someone understood me.

Our fingers touched. His eyes widened with surprise—but not displeasure.

Oh man, what was I doing? That was on the wrong side of the line between flirting and friendly. Considering I was supposed to be at an engagement party—maybe even my own engagement party—I should not have been sharing flirty compliments with anyone. Especially not the enemy.

I took a step back, but that was as far as I got before the music shifted, signaling something happening up front.

I turned just in time to see Sheridan climb onto the stage. She strode to the center where a microphone had been placed, a perfect smile on her lips. "A toast!" she said, lifting her glass of sparkling cider. "Could we get Prince Owen and the sisters up here? Please?"

People turned to look at me. A dozen faces stared with expectation, some moonlight pale, some tan and familiar.

The sisters. That included me. Right.

I squared my shoulders, taking a deep breath to try to slow my racing heart. The vampire walked me to the stage, and the crowd parted for us, letting me step through without having to bump any shoulders. I kept my eyes open for this horrible vampire prince I was supposed to marry. If he looked anything like his father—severe, austere, and scary as all get out—he wouldn't be hard to pick from the crowd.

My new friend gave me a hand up on stage. I took it, though only to avoid the commentary if I'd refused. I gave him a look that hopefully conveyed *Go Away!* before turning away from him and making my way toward Sheridan. The lights were so bright that they warmed my shoulders immediately. I pumped my hands open and closed as my palms clammed up.

I stepped into line, shoulder to shoulder with Regan and felt someone brush up beside me on my left. I looked over and froze.

My vampire stranger stood beside me, his attention on the crowd. No one said anything about it and I realized with slow, frigid awareness that he was here because he was supposed to be. And suddenly, everything about him was commanding. He faced the crowd with a charismatic smirk, opening his arms wide. “Thank you so much for having me here,” he said into the microphone.

I flinched—an icy shiver rocking through me as I understood but struggled to find a reason to be wrong.

“No way,” I whispered.

As if I’d spoken only to him, my vampire turned and winked at me before continuing his formal hello and offering up a toast to the crowd. All I could do was stand and listen, numb, as I went through the motions of raising my glass and sipping appropriately to my own—or Regan’s—impending marriage.

I couldn’t believe it.

The friend I’d made in the forest—my vampire—was the evil, scary, monstrous Prince Owen. And I had about three seconds to decide what I was going to do about it.

..*

The story continues in Bitter Beloved, book 2 in the Bitterroot Series!

ABOUT THE AUTHORS

Heather Hildenbrand was born and raised in a small town in northern Virginia where she was homeschooled through high school. (She's only slightly socially awkward as a result.) She writes paranormal and contemporary romance with plenty of abs and angst. Her most frequent hobbies are riding motorcycles and avoiding killer slugs.

Find out more at heatherhildenbrand.com.

SM Reine writes urban fantasy and paranormal romance. She collects swords, cat hair, and typewriters (which she does use for writing!). She can usually be found working on her treadmill desk at midnight while her four black cats glare disapprovingly.

Find out more at www.smreine.com.

Also by Heather Hildenbrand

O Face: Is Summerville's most eligible bachelor hot enough to melt the ice princess herself?

Whisper: A New Adult Fantasy Romance full of loss and true love and justice served. There's also a hot Cherokee warrior involved.

A Risk Worth Taking: A New Adult Contemporary Romance with southern charm and a hippie farmer capable of swoon and heartbreak in the same breath.

Dirty Blood: A Young Adult Paranormal Romance about a girl who falls in love with a werewolf, only to find out she's a Hunter, born and bred to kill the very thing she means to save.

Imitation: A Young Adult SciFi Romance with life or death choices and a conspiracy so deep, even a motorcycle-riding bodyguard can't pull you out.